Praise for *trans(re)lating house one*

"Poupeh Missaghi is so keenly attuned to the frequencies of city life that reading her novel of Tehran felt like a revelation. In fragments layered over one another, moments are extended, lives are resurrected, lovers meet, and many questions are asked. Which of the dead do we honor and why? Whose stories do we listen to, and why do we listen to them, and are we ever really listening? *trans(re)lating house one* is a searching, brilliant novel completely unlike anything I've ever read."

—*Shuchi Saraswat, Brookline Booksmith*

"In a series of pieces that constitute a haunting, harrowing whole, Poupeh Missaghi gives us one of the more close, contemporary glimpses of Iran to reach readers' eyes here. Coming out of Iran's tumultuous 2009 election, this book looks at disappearance, witness, perseverance, voice, loss, presence, absence, and longing in the hearts, souls, and lives of people there. The narratives here shatter one moment, shimmer another, narrating as stories will, yet also interrogating the nature of the narration. What language is this? Why this language? Why these stories, for whose eyes and what purpose? These and other questions cast, the stories told here make for a compelling chronicle of telling power, of necessary testimony. What a book this is."

—*Rick Simonson, Elliott Bay Book Company*

trans(re)lating house one

Poupeh Missaghi

COFFEE HOUSE PRESS
Minneapolis
2020

Coffee House Press books are available to the trade through our primary distributor, Consortium Book Sales & Distribution, cbsd.com or (800) 283-3572. For personal orders, catalogs, or other information, write to info@coffeehousepress.org.

Coffee House Press is a nonprofit literary publishing house. Support from private foundations, corporate giving programs, government programs, and generous individuals helps make the publication of our books possible. We gratefully acknowledge their support in detail in the back of this book.

LIBRARY OF CONGRESS CATALOGING-IN-PUBLICATION DATA

Names: Missaghi, Poupeh, author.
Title: Trans(re)lating house one / Poupeh Missaghi.
Description: Minneapolis : Coffee House Press, 2020.
Identifiers: LCCN 2019015717 (print) | LCCN 2019016843 (ebook) |
    ISBN 9781566895736 (ebook) | ISBN 9781566895651 (trade pbk.)
Subjects: LCSH: Iranians—Fiction. | Tehran (Iran)—Social conditions—Fiction.
Classification: LCC PS3613.I84475 (ebook) | LCC PS3613.I84475 T73 2020 (print) |
    DDC 813/.6—dc23
LC record available at https://lccn.loc.gov/2019015717

PRINTED IN THE UNITED STATES OF AMERICA

26 25 24 23 22 21 20 19   1 2 3 4 5 6 7 8

Parts of this work are based on true (hi)stories, but I make no claim about the factual accuracy of my trans(re)lations of the events, places, individuals, and peoples.

trans(re)lating house one

I want to start in the after: the aftershock, the aftermath, the afterworld. I want to start with the slippery, the intangible. I want to start with the impenetrable, the incomprehensible.
I want to start with the world of dreams.
But I will not reveal it all now. I will not tell the whole now, because the whole only becomes the whole in parts, in conversation with the parts, dispersed in time, in space, arrived at only through passage. Suffice it to say for now that dreams matter, that they are the heart of the matter translated from one plane to another, one language to another, from the conscious to the unconscious back to the conscious. They remain illegible. They carry the secret.

She does not remember how it all began, why and when. Perhaps it was during one of the weekly gallery hops or as she followed the news of the statues or on her bus ride the day she went to meet one of the sculptors. Perhaps it all began long before, on a day her memory doesn't even hold on to.

I do remember how it all began, why and when, though vaguely. The way I remember the origins of all stories, all books. It always begins with a search. A search, in this case, for the meanings of what came before the dreams.

It also started with an obsession with Roberto Bolaño and "The Part about the Crimes" in *2666*. It started in Selah Saterstrom's hermeneutics class in the winter of 2012, in which I drew a tarot card, a Ten of Wands, which served as a prompt for writing. I remember that image not as a man holding sprouting sticks and reaping his rewards, but as a man carrying pointed burdens on his back.

Outside the window the city moves. She is on a bus. In the women-only section. She knows the city, and she doesn't know the city. She sees the city outside the bus windows, and she reads the city in the newspaper on her lap. The city is disappearing. Dying. The city is resisting. Being born. It dies every second. It comes back to life every second after. The city keeps reappearing. The city is gaining more presence. Inside her. A very loud silence. The city is disintegrating. Outside her. Noises. A map. Create a map before the city falls apart. She hears a ghostly voice and turns around. Nobody is saying anything.

I desire for her to create a map that can reinvent itself every time the city does. A secret map, a personal map, an internal map, a map in words, a map in tongues. Today the city is not what it was yesterday. Tomorrow it won't be what it is today. The map needs to be continuously rebirthed. New places. New names. New roads. New lines. Like cells. Like veins. Of her body. Of my body. Of the bodies of the women and men on the bus. Of the bodies of the women and men outside the bus. Of the bodies in the city, making the text. The map of the city is to be drawn with words. The map is the text. The text is the map. The text is the city. But even that will not remain stable. Even that will be forever changing. The text breathes. The text grows. The text decomposes. The city grows and dies and dies and grows. The city decomposes. The city breathes.

She turns around. Everyone is looking outside. Everyone is looking inside. Nobody is saying anything.

The city is losing its statues. I read about this online. It feels surreal, as if nonfiction is already fiction. I want her to map the city, to follow the trail of the lost statues. The statues disappear. The public spaces once dedicated to their bodies remain void. The city has more space, less space. I want her to find the bronze bodies. Find the bodies. But no one can find the bodies. Once they disappear, they are gone. No matter how fast I search, she searches, no matter how hard, the city will remain one step ahead.

But what if we're looking in the wrong city? On the wrong map? I desire for her to draw a map of the city that is a womb, that is a breath, that is a world, that is nothing, that is everything: a map not to show us the path but to lead us away from the path, a map of the city that is a body, a body sexing, defecating, coughing, biting, spitting, suffocating, caressing, listening, hearing, speaking, a map of the city that is, the city that is not.

What if we're looking for the monuments on the wrong map? What if we looked for the lost bodies on a different map instead? I want us to draw the map that . . . draw the map that . . . the map that . . .

Traffic has come to a halt. The bus is stuck. Not moving. Idling.

Outside, people have gathered. Are waiting. She looks out to see.

Other women too. Someone calls out to the bus driver to open the

doors. He does. Some leave. Out the front door. Out the back door.

She cranes her neck.

A cow is slaughtered in the middle of the square. She sees a big

banner covering several store signs. "We welcome a new police

mission for social order," it says. We are the store owners. We are

they. They welcome the new mission. They welcome the order.

They have the cow killed. They have the cow sacrificed. A sacrifice

for gratitude, for thankfulness. The city will be cleansed of addicts,

vagrants, beggars, peddlers, of the vicious and immoral. Traffic

laws will be better implemented. The new mission will improve the

lives of the citizens and the city. Better days will come.

The city will become pure.

Sacrifice for purity.

Sacrifice of one body for another. One of flesh. The other of brick and cement and asphalt and glass, of gray and gray and green and red and orange and green and gray and gray and black.

Sacrifice as ritual.

Rituals need to be carried out in open spaces. Rituals define public identities. Rituals need to have witnesses. They are symbolic, deliver a message. To the gods. To the people.

What does it mean to sacrifice bodies for a greater cause? To perform rituals to create meaning? To symbolize life? Or death?

The cow is sacrificed in the middle of the day, in the middle
of the square. The cars and human beings come to a halt to watch
the cow die, to welcome a new era of social order. Bus passengers
stare. People gather on the green patch in the middle of the
square and stare. The cow lies in the middle of the road. The cow
bleeds. The cow breathes. The cow is a corpse. The corpse is too
heavy. Shopkeepers cannot move it into a van. Onlookers join to
help. Shopkeepers and onlookers cannot move the cow that is
now the corpse into a van. They gather. They touch, each a corner
of the body. They try. They hold on to. They hold their breath.
They push. The corpse remains on the road. In the middle of the
square, a fountain continues to breathe water into the air. Water
rises up and drops down. A tow truck is called. Life comes to a
halt before the corpse of the cow. The sacrifice. The ritual. The
cow. The people. The cars. Together. Entangled. The narrow path
around the body, kept open to traffic, is now a knot of cars and
buses and motorbikes and people.
The sound of horns. The murmurs and shouts of humans. The
silence of the animal. The silence of the trees and the crows
standing watch. The knot cannot be untied until the corpse is
moved away. The passersby pause for a moment then move on,

or they pause for a moment and stay for another, or they move to the center to see, to understand, and then try to find a way out or decide to stay a bit longer before moving on. The cow corpse begins to rot on the asphalt in the square

An hour later the tow truck arrives, and the driver and the shopkeepers and the men get together and, with the help of a metal chain, move the corpse from the pavement up behind the truck. Traffic officers open a path through the crowd. The truck moves slowly away. The water continues to flow from the fountain. The cow is gone. The blood of the cow dries on the asphalt under the sun. The crows sing and fly away. The trees continue to stand still.

Missing Statue (13): The Calf

Location: The calf, along with the parent cow, had lived in front of the school of veterinary medicine at the University of Tehran since the day the school opened.
Date Gone Missing: Spring 2010
The cow remains standing.

"Works of public art involve preparation, realisation, potential evaluation and the everyday reality thereof. Apart from public *space,* it is therefore important to acknowledge that public art also involves public *time.* Both the artwork and the space are [moreover] in interplay with the art engager (i.e. the subject), and hence there is a subject-object-space-time nexus. This nexus implies that elements of subject, object, space and time exist by the grace of each other. Such a nexus is thus more-than-just-human, although it rests in the eye of the art engager" (Zebracki 2015).

Missing Statue (12): The Foal

Location: The foal, along with the parent horse, had lived in front of the school of veterinary medicine at the University of Tehran.
Date Gone Missing: Spring 2010
The horse remains standing.

Missing Statue (11): The Wagtail Gives Life
to Seven Babies, One Is a Nightingale

Abstract
Location: Esteghlal Park
Date Gone Missing: Spring 2010

"Public art may be seen as an intermediating agency in social culture and thus as a powerful yet elusive player in spatial politics (Deutsche 1996; Kester 1998). Its existence is often linked to institutional and policy contexts" (Zebracki 2015).

What holds true about the existence of public art holds true for its annihilation as well.

Missing Statue (10): Bust

Abstract
Location: Artists Park
Date Gone Missing: Spring 2010

Missing Statue (9): Life

Abstract
Location: Artists Park
Date Gone Missing: Spring 2010

"'The work, the ideal, dreamt work, does not exist without its stage, its support, its subjectile, its earth. The 'stage' of the visual work of art is double: 1) the work (painting, photo, installation, sculpture, etc.) is born in a genealogy, in a vast time, a sort of library-landscape which remembers-and-forgets, which keeps and brings back to life all the previous works. 2) The other stage is its genetic geography, its spatial context, its urban, political site" (Cixous 2006).

Missing Statue (8): Avicenna

World-famous Persian polymath
Date of Birth: 980
Date of Death: 1037
Location: Behjat Abad Park
Date Gone Missing: Spring 2010

Missing Statue (7): Sattar Khan

Also known as the National Commander, one
of the two leaders of Iran's Constitutional
Revolution
Date of Birth: 1866
Date of Death: 1914
Location: Sattar Khan Street
Date Gone Missing: Spring 2010

Missing Statue (6): Bagher Khan

Also known as the National Chief, one of the
two leaders of Iran's Constitutional Revolution
Date of Birth: 1861
Date of Death: 1916
Location: Shahr Ara Street
Date Gone Missing: Around the same time as
Sattar Khan, spring 2010

What are the ethical implications of raising monuments for a movement's dead? Of creating celebrities of them?
Who decides who should become a celebrity in death?
Isn't it disrespectful even to use the word "celebrity" for the dead of a movement?

Missing Statue (5): Mohammad Sanie Khatam

Master inlay artist
Date of Birth: 1891
Date of Death: Unknown
Location: Mellat Park
Date Gone Missing: Spring 2010

Missing Statue (4): Shahriar

Poet who wrote poems in Persian and Azeri. The date of his death is commemorated as the National Day of Persian Poetry and Literature in Iran.
Date of Birth: 1906
Date of Death: 1988
Location: The statue had primarily lived in front of Vahdat Hall, on Shahriar Boulevard, but was moved to its location in front of Shahr Theater a year before its disappearance.
Date Gone Missing: Spring 2010

Missing Statue (3): Mohammad Mo'in

Professor of Persian literature and compiler of
the *Mo'in Encyclopedia*
Date of Birth: 1918
Date of Death: 1971
Location: Ostad Mo'in Boulevard
Date Gone Missing: Spring 2010

Missing Statue (2): Ali Shariati

Sociologist, historian, theologist, political
activist, and author
Date of Birth: 1933
Date of Death: 1977
Location: Shariati Park
Date Gone Missing: Spring 2010

Why this persistence in commemorating? In remembering?
In fighting forgetfulness?
Is selectivity the enemy of remembrance or is it the very definition
of remembrance?
Can we remember what we once forgot?
Can we forget what we once remembered? What we once
memorized? What we once knew? What we once experienced?
How much can we forget?
How much is enough?
When should we stop? Commemorating? Remembering?
Reminding? Blaming? Missing? Mourning? Forgetting? Inviting
to forget? Inviting to forgive? Forgiving?
Who should decide?
How can we free ourselves from the past while honoring it?

Missing Statue (1): Mother and Child

Location: San'at Square
Date Gone Missing: Spring 2010

The statues went missing from public spaces in Tehran in the spring of 2010, in the aftermath of the events.

The visibility of the statues—in plain sight—suggests the existence of witnesses: ordinary citizens, police officers, cameras. The size and weight of the statues suggest intricate planning and use of heavy machinery for their removal.

The media covered the news. Only at the beginning. That's why I was able to read about them on the other side of the world. Authorities promised investigations. Only at the beginning. No investigative journalism was carried out. Or very little. Perhaps it was not allowed. Or it was but remained unpublished. No further police investigation was carried out. Or it was. No results were ever reported to the public.

I imagine her on a search for the statues.

Where to search? How to search?

Traffic moves. Little by little. She checks her watch. She is late for her meeting with one of the sculptors. The light turns red. The bus driver opens the door, though the bus has not yet reached the stop. Some people get in. The women's section in the back gets busier than the men's in the front. The new passengers ask the others to push farther toward the back. Her head on the not-so-clean glass of the bus, she shifts her gaze from the cars outside to the women inside to the ads and handwritten notices on the walls. Note the new ticket prices for the following routes. Provide exact change. Use your commuter card. Keep the bus clean. Women lose themselves in their phones or in small talk. Ticket prices for private buses have been raised by the same people running public buses. People prefer public buses; they are much cheaper, but there's a limited number of them. People have to take buses. People cannot afford to take cabs. People cannot sit in cabs stuck for hours in traffic. People do not have access to metro lines for every destination. People should stop using their cars. People cannot . . . People do not . . . People should not . . . People could . . . People should . . . It is six in the evening. This is a private bus. She has heard enough complaints for the day.

She adjusts the earphones in her ears under her scarf and turns the music up to block out the voices of the people and the public radio. The light turns green. Traffic moves forward. Little by little. At the fifth stop, the woman walks in and pushes her way through the crowd that jams the aisle between the seats, pulling behind her a girl who tries to keep pace. The woman and the girl find a spot to stand, squeezed in between the other fatigued passengers a few steps to the right of her seat. The next time the doors of the bus open and close, she looks out to make sure she is not missing her stop. When she looks back inside, the woman and the girl are no longer in the aisle. But they are not gone. They are sitting in the seats in front of her, facing her. The two older women have apparently left. She wonders whether the girl is the woman's. She wonders whether the girl is one of those rented out to create a certain profile for beggars: a parent in need with a child to be pitied. To create a certain profile for givers: a soul pained by injustice, a person generous enough to reach into a purse or a center console for extra cash to hand out. She closes her eyes to the public around her, opens her ears to the melodies privately entering her body, but it is useless. She is too curious to not look at them.

She opens her eyes as soon as the bus starts to leave the stop. The woman moves in her seat. She notices she is holding another child, a baby that can't be more than a few months old, in ragged, dust-covered swaddling clothes, in a back wrap. The baby's cheeks, black and rosy at the same time, are the cheeks of a wanderer by force rather than by choice, carried around the streets all day long. The baby fumbles with the hair under the mother's veil while gripping a piece of stale bread. She stares at them, stares until the woman finally looks back at her, stares only a moment longer before turning her gaze away from them and toward the window. The traffic has come to a halt once again. She turns her head again, looks back inside. They are gone, some other woman is in her seat, an old woman in her girl's. The doors have once again been opened. She looks toward the aisle, searching. She glimpses the little girl's back as she's pulled past the seats, through bodies hanging on to metal bars in the middle of the bus, almost not bodies, almost just clothes, steeped in sweat and pollution and fatigue. The girl is pulled. The doors are closed. And then . . . they are gone. The girl. The mother. The baby. Lost among others who try to find a way in or out through the mass of bodies in the bus. The women inside push closer and closer toward the back to open some space for the new passengers. It is rush hour. She comes out of her daze and jumps to her feet. She doesn't want to lose them. It's almost impossible to pass through all the jammed bodies to get to the door. She calls out to the driver to open the door before the bus gains speed. Men turn around in their section at the front, agitated, curious. She hears her voice echo back toward her through the bus. Mouths don't open. Lips don't move. The shout echoes. As if each and every one of the passengers, men and women, is repeating her request. The words are passed from woman to woman to girl to man to man to old man to young man and finally to the driver. The door opens, the bus already beyond the stop, blocking the traffic behind it. The air outside is not fresh. She stumbles down the metal steps and rushes away from the bus.

Re: the right alignment of the text, if you're curious.
This is foreign territory. Its map needs to be foreign. I want it to
make you stumble. I want you to be disrupted when you arrive
here, feel some discomfort, feel out of place.
The language of the city is Persian. My first language is Persian.
Persian is written from right to left. I want to hold on to its
presence. Even if only as a ghost.
I want to acknowledge the Otherness of both the territory and
the language to you, make them visible, and celebrate them as
I translate the city and its people into this other language of mine.

Outside the bus, in the street, she finds them. In the crowd of pedestrians, the girl following the woman, the baby moving up and down against her slightly curved back. She follows. The girl stops and looks back. As if she has sensed a shadow. The mother keeps walking. She, with a beggar veil wrapped around her shoulder that reveals her cheaply highlighted hair, she, in ragged flip-flops blackened by city soot, walks with residues of grace. Each time the girl stops and looks around, she, at a distance, pauses, only for a moment, and glances at her watch, pretending that she has nothing to do with them. She thinks to herself that she should probably hail a cab and get to her meeting. But the thought lingers only for a second. The distance between them grows. She starts walking faster. She follows them all the way down the street, through alleys that keep getting narrower, shabbier, into a square where there's a bazaar. The tiny shops are starting to close up for the day. They're so small that there's only room for some shelves packed with random goods and a makeshift counter in front, so small that the shopkeepers are forced to stand outside, in front of their treasures—broken TVs, old radio transmitters, trays of ill-matched cutlery, the remainders of old tea sets, car equipment, stereos, abandoned locks and keys. Relics of homes long disappeared.

Relics stolen and sold. The men stand in groups of two or three, drinking tea from greasy glasses, cigarettes clinging to their fingers or smoke-blackened lips. They shoot her discreet and not-so-discreet glances. The square is a men's space. Their property. But she can handle their gaze. It is the gaze of their merchandise that feels heavy to her, heavy enough to make her aware of her own body's movements along the walls as she approaches the three bodies she has been following. The woman stops in front of one of the larger shops. She stops in front of a newsstand in the middle of the square that sells snacks, beverages, cigarettes, and some tabloid magazines and sports newspapers.

She pretends to browse while watching the family from the corner of her eye. The woman talks to a shopkeeper. The two seem to know each other. The shopkeeper's hand plays with his mustache as he looks her up and down: as if he wants to pierce her veil, her clothes, her skin. The girl holds the mother's hand more tightly, clings to her, not allowing the mother to let her go. The baby is dozing off on the mother's back, his head tipping from time to time.

The shopkeeper and the mother keep chatting. The newsstand vendor eyes her eyeing them suspiciously. The woman unwraps the baby, still asleep, and hands him to the man. The man embraces him and kisses his cheek. She picks up a chocolate bar and asks the vendor for a pack of cigarettes and a lighter. The mother sits down in front of the girl, whispers something in her ear, kisses her, and puts her hand in the man's. The girl lets her hand be taken, as if she knows this man, as if she knows this ritual. The girl becomes a statue next to the man. He doesn't say anything to her. She doesn't look up at him. The mother walks away without looking back.

She pays hurriedly and carries on following her. The girl gives her a reassuring look as she passes them by. The girl smiles and glances at the baby and the man. The man takes her and the baby into the shop. The mother turns a corner. She wonders what she should do if she gets hold of her. She wonders what excuse she should give the sculptor she was supposed to meet. She wonders what she needs to say, what she needs to ask. She turns the corner. She enters a dead end.

She comes face to face with the woman, who has been waiting for her. She looks at her with eyes that are as wild as a cat's, as frightened as a cornered cat's. She looks at her and says nothing. She checks around to make sure they are alone. She takes a piece of paper and pen from her bag, scribbles something down, and places the paper on the pavement with a little stone to hold it there. Then she stands up, takes a few steps, comes closer. She reaches out and caresses her cheek, holding her hand there for what feels like a long time but is not, before walking away.

She breathes in deeply and picks up the paper. It reads, "Keep looking for the bodies."

I imagine her standing there, holding on to the traces of the woman's touch, the warmth in her cheek, the trembling in her body, the questions in her mind. I imagine her lost and confused but surprisingly calm. I imagine her reading the note. I imagine her reading but not really understanding. It is a long journey: from reading the words to reading the in-between of the words. I imagine her continuing her search for the bodies frozen in time, in art. I want to let her. She needs the search for the statues to go on for a while. But I know. And I know that she, too, cannot *not* know, even though she doesn't know, not really. And I want you to know as well. That there are other bodies too. Bodies that I am going to search for, while she is busy searching for her own bodies.

What is in the body that offers closure?

What is it about the body that makes families left with no body to bury or mourn continue to look for and demand the body?

Why does telling the stories of the bodies, missing or buried, seem to be the next best thing for survivors who have not been able to reclaim the bodies of their loved ones?

Can narratives tell stories the way bodies do?

What is in a story that makes it like a body?

If the story is written but not told, told but not received, received but not understood, understood but not appreciated, then is the story worth anything at all?

How does a story that needs to circulate in order to live become a body that needs to be buried in order to live?

Is the story the body, or is the body the story? Are they strangers who need to meet so that a larger story can be born and narrated?

What bodies to follow? Why these bodies?

What point of entry should I adopt for resurrecting these bodies? What angle should I take? What point of view? What voice? What form? What setting?

At what time should I enter these (hi)stories?

For what times should I tell them?

Corpse (1)

Age: 23
Gender: Male
Date Shot: 25 Khordad 1388 / 15 June 2009
Place Shot: Tehran
Date of Death: 18 Aban 1390 / 9 November 2011
Place of Death: Boston
Time of Death: Unknown
Cause of Death: Shrapnel residue in brain tissue
Date of Burial: 30 Dey 1390 / 20 January 2012
Place of Burial: Berlin

Silence. Protest. Scattered slogans.
Armed forces marching on the rooftop of a Basij base.
The protest continues.
Slogans are repeated. Shouted in louder voices.
Tear gas. Bullets. Snipers.
Blood. Bodies.
He rushes to help. He unwraps the scarf around his neck and sits down to tie it around the wound on another protester's leg.
More bullets.
When he stands and turns to call for his friend, he is shot in the head. In the forehead.
Blood. Ground. Darkness.
He is taken to the hospital.
He is taken into surgery immediately. Hands. Tubes. Gloves. Instruments.
Pieces of shrapnel are taken out. Pieces remain in the brain.
Bandages.
He falls into a coma.
Family unaware of his location.

His parents are divorced. The father is said to be affiliated with regime forces. The father and son are said to have been distant. The mother, a housewife. Five sisters, all older. One brother, deceased, a martyr of the Iran–Iraq War.

The family looks for him. The mother and sisters. Prison inmate lists. He is not on any of them.

The medical examiner's office. Prison morgues. The sister checks dozens of crushed faces and dead bodies. To no avail. His body is not found.

Hospitals. Hospital officials tell the sister, in hushed voices, that corpses are removed by the police. No name. No identity. No record. No evidence.

After the surgery, he remains in a hospital as a man injured in an accident. Fears of his being found, arrested, and removed. Fears of the hospital staff being charged with cooperation with the opposition forces.

The staff wants the tubes disconnected. The doctor will not allow it. The body lies there, silent.

The family searches.

He comes out of the coma. A month or so later.

Symptoms: Memory loss. Unable to control the excretion of feces. Needs tubes. Unable to talk properly. Partially paralyzed.

He regains part of his memory. He cannot yet speak. The doctor provides him with a pen and paper. He writes down numbers. The phone number of one of his sisters.

The family finds him.

For his safety, he is immediately discharged.

At home, he rests. As if a baby, helpless, he is cared for. Family. Doctors. Speech therapy. Physiotherapy. A second surgery. On the brain.

The family moves. For safety. For peace of mind. So that they can pay his hospital bills.

Seven to eight months later, he is partially recovered. He still suffers amnesia. He regains some speech. He still suffers seizures.

The family arranges for him to leave the country. He is a witness. Of the silent protest. Of the silent bullets.

Destination: Turkey.

He goes to the movies, to internet cafés, speaks and laughs, falls silent from time to time, suffers headaches, does not receive needed medical attention.

Months later. Refugee status accepted. He hopes to go to Germany, where he has family. The UN offers him refugee status in the U.S. The family requests to send someone with him to care for him there. Request is denied.

Destination: Boston.

The son arrives in Boston. Alone. Penniless. Some support from other immigrants. Limited medical care for six months. No special care. Nothing after six months. He repeatedly loses sensation in his limbs, suffers seizures, and has to go to the hospital. He is not admitted. He cannot afford to pay. He is told he might not have long to live. He grows depressed.

He hopes to eventually leave the U.S., to join a sister who left Iran after the protests, after the search, after the pain, who now lives in Malaysia.

He lives eight months in Boston.

He chats regularly with the sister in Malaysia. One day she doesn't find him on the other side of the screen.

Absence.

Silence.

He has been taken to the hospital. She finds out through his friends.

Silence.

Death.

An autopsy is performed on the body. He has had a brain hemorrhage.

The mother wishes to see the second son she has lost before he is buried. The family does not want to risk transferring the corpse back to Iran. Fear of the body being confiscated. Fear of complications for the funeral and the survivors.

The mortuary cooler in Boston is his home for countless days.

His body rests alone.

The mother cannot travel to the u.s. The mother wishes to see her son one last time. The mother wants her son to be buried where he has family. Germany.

His body decomposes.

The German government facilitates the transfer of the body. The German government issues a visa for the mother.

The body travels. The mother travels.

After about two months in the solitary confinement of a cooler in Boston, the body is buried in Berlin. Red tulips. White roses and lilies. Pale orchids. A light-brown casket. Family and acquaintances and activists. A black-and-white picture. Of him smiling, young and full of life.

The family remains silent until his death. Fear of his arrest. Fear of his torture. Fear of losing him once again.

Following his death, they speak.

The sister living in Malaysia speaks and tells the story. She continues to follow up on his case with human-rights organizations.

Within the borders of Iran, the family announces a fake cause of death in order to hold a ceremony.

They mourn a son killed in a made-up accident, not a son lost to bullets. They mourn and recite his name in hushed voices. He is not to be talked about. In Turkey, refugees who knew him from his time there hold a small ceremony. Wonder what his destiny would have been if his request to be sent to Germany had been accepted.

The mother speaks. A while later. The mother cries. Speaks of his wishes in life: to become a diver, to work on large ships, to take care of his mother. Of him telling her on that protest day that he was going to see a movie with friends, going to see his father later to get some money, going to stay at his aunt's afterward. Of finding out in the small hours of the day that he didn't go to his aunt's. Of later learning the details of the protest. Of the search. Of the prayers and cries. Of him contacting them. After the coma. Of the thirty-six baton scars on his back. Of his bloody clothes sticking to his skin. Of him surviving only because he was an athlete. Of sending him abroad to save him from any further harm. Of his being sent to the u.s. Of the rejection of his sister's request to travel with him. Of their connection through the internet. Of his refugee pension being too little, too late. Of her sending him money. Of his hard life, what he ate, what he wore. Of his being alone, his loneliness, his homesickness. Of his medication. Of his laughter. Of her long-distance phone card running out of minutes. Of telling him she'd buy a new card and call him later so he didn't have to pay. Of being given the news. Of that next call never happening. Of the decision to bury him in Berlin. Of not wanting her child's body to be displaced in Iran. Of wishing they had stayed together in Turkey for what remained of his life. The mother speaks. The mother cries.

"My elder son went to the battlefield to defend the soil of Iran and was killed. But I could not bury his younger brother in Iran's soil," the mother says. He was the youngest child, beloved by all. He is survived by his mother, his father, and his sisters.

I want to hold a moment of silence here. Out of respect. In memory.

Re: not naming the corpses.

"Do not murmur the names of the dead because if you murmur the names of the dead you will ruin the poetry of death" (Borzutzky 2011).

"It feels different to mourn something without naming its name" (Nelson 2005).

"And let us pray for the nameless corpses . . . The corpses are everyone and they are alone and alive in the grass and the sand and the forests and in our nostalgia for graves and tombstones and flowers that mark the memory of those bodies that once had names. And let us pray for the nameless corpses but let us not name them, says a body on a page of mutilated trees. . . . And the bodies ask the readers to pray with them. And the bodies tell the readers that by simply turning the pages they will be uttering the prayers for the dead" (Borzutzky 2011).

Please keep turning the pages, reader. Please keep praying for the dead. With me, with them.

corpse (14)
unconfirmed reports

They go down the stairs that lead to the gallery. Some people are leaving. At the door there is a sign that reads, "Private Show. By Invitation Only." They could be denied entry. They don't have invitations. But the artist is at the door saying good-bye to some guests, and when she sees them, she tells the doorman to let them in. She knows her from years back. She is hoping the sculptor will show up for the opening. She knows he knows the artist. She is hoping she can ask him a few questions. The hall is crowded. Young men and women, perhaps a new generation of artists, perhaps non-artists simply enamored with artistic milieus, mingle with older artists. A woman looks for more catalogs. A handsome older man takes a cup of tea from the tray the server is passing around.

"My Period," the pamphlet reads.

On the walls, in ornate golden frames: A menstrual pad with a cockroach in the middle. A pad with several bloodstains here and there. A pad with the ash from a cigarette. A pad with a safety pin in the middle. A pad with a pen cap. A pad with embroidery all around. A pad with the picture of a woman in the middle. A pad pasted over old, yellowing newspapers. A pad surrounded by words. A pad soaked in blood.

She and a friend walk around the gallery, saying hi to people they know, discussing the pieces on the walls. She suddenly sees a face she is certain she knows, but she can't remember where from. She pauses and stares, unconsciously but so intensely that the other woman feels the weight of her gaze. The woman smiles. She smiles back and steps through the gliding French doors to the gallery courtyard. She can't remember her name.

Several people are sitting around a table on seats made of tree trunks, smoking and drinking tea. People look her up and down. On the corner of the table, a tray of dates and sweets. Two kids are running around the empty fenced-in swimming pool. She looks around to see if the sculptor is out in the courtyard, but he is not. Talking to others and trying to decide which gallery to head to after this, she can't stop thinking about the familiar face of the woman inside. And then she remembers.

The film. An homage to the women of the land. Never released. Made with novice actors and actresses. Episodic. Each episode the story of a female character dealing with one problem or another. Personal problems. Social contexts. The cast of each episode knowing only about their own episode, not about the movie as a whole, not about the other women. In the final credits, the only name revealed is that of the director.

Woven together, the larger picture could be deemed too bleak, vile, untrue. Could cause them to run into trouble with the officials.

So the women appearing in front of the camera remain unaware
of the presence of the others, or pretend to be. An unknowing.
A silence. For protection.
And that is what she, too, does, for now: she pretends. Even
though she, the one who made their words appear on the screen
in the language of the Other, has seen them all, knows them
all, has watched the pieces come together to create this
one mass, one story.

Each woman is part of a community. Each has been and is alone. Each helps herself. Each helps the others. All support the greater project. In hushed voices. In obliterated identities. In search of a new identity through art. Losing the self to find the self through art. Losing the self to create a larger self.

A film about the daily lives and struggles of women might or might not be screened where it was inspired, where it was produced. Its permits depend on the who and the when, on the winds of politics. To find an audience, it might need to be sent to one international festival or another. But international festivals might have their own issues. Most often looking for certain narratives of backwardness and victimhood, they pay attention to sociopolitics instead of aesthetics, *instead of* not *alongside*. A neo-orientalism bolstering the existing narrative of the Other who needs to be pitied, or feared. Such is the case in literature too. Certain narratives, certain representations. Only a pretention to inclusivity, to diversity, to equality.

Think about the burdens of the creator, the artist.

Do the motives behind the artwork/writing have their intended effects on the audience/reader?

Why do we imagine a narrative of political events to always have political motives?

It is naive to even imagine that a narrative from this time, this place, this event, this people, this regime, written by a woman who does not feel belonging within any one border, within any one language, within any one definition, would be read as anything but political, especially in this language of the Other, in this land of the Other.

How do the political implications of the work change as a result of changes in the linguistic, cultural, and political context surrounding it? As a result of the spatial and the temporal context surrounding it? Can political narratives change the political climate?

What is the meaning of "political"? What makes something political? Can anything be truly apolitical?

Are things political by nature, or is it narrating them, speaking them, writing them that makes them political?

Or is it reading them that makes them political?

She walks back inside the gallery, visits different rooms to see if the sculptor has made an appearance. The woman is sipping tea and staring into the gold frame that embraces a blood-soaked pad. The woman doesn't know her, isn't aware that she worked on the film. She knows the woman, no, she doesn't know the woman, but she knows something about the woman: her character in the film, her part, her story. In one scene in her episode, she sits alone in a gallery, a single woman staring at a piece of art and praying that she is pregnant with the illicit child of her lover. She checks her cell phone from time to time, perhaps wondering whether or not to text the lover to give him the news, or perhaps waiting to hear back from the clinic before taking any further steps.

She sits next to the actress and joins her in staring at the pad. She pretends she's just another stranger in the room, but then the actress, still staring straight ahead at the frame, begins speaking to her, or herself: Why do we need to bleed?

Her friend comes inside to tell her they need to leave. The sculptor is not coming, she says. The actress looks at the two of them. She smiles at the actress and murmurs a good-bye as she gets up to leave. Still sitting, the actress nods graciously, then turns to continue staring at the pad.

At a café later that evening, four women sit at a table. They order herbal teas. One woman has brought some homemade halva. I don't know why, but today I had an urge to make halva. I'm not sure which dead it's for. Have some and say a prayer for whomever you wish, or for all the dead you know and don't know, or for our own future dead selves, she says half-jokingly. On the walls there are black-and-white pictures of neighborhoods around the city. She ignores the halva and stands to look at the images. They are new, she realizes, manipulated to look old. The two young men and a young woman sitting at the next table keep laughing and texting. On the walls, branches and utility poles and gates and windows and cabs and squares and public art and traffic lights and brick walls and newsstands and fruits and birds and construction sites and motorbikes and meat hanging from hooks in front of a butcher shop and flower girls and policemen and trash cans and boulevards and cul-de-sacs and ATMs and cafés and store signs and a mother and child and students and, and, and, and, and. On the back wall, on the other side of the staircase they've just come up, is a map of the city, not framed, adhered to the wall with dozens of wads of chewed gum. The map looks blurred and is illegible. She gets as close as she can to the railing. The map is many maps of the city, the norths and souths and easts and wests overlaying one another, the dates in the upper right corner turning into a year in a future that may or may not arrive or in a past that has disappeared without any trace, the streets and alleys and highways converging into a labyrinth with no entrance or exit in time or space. There are several red pins dotting the map, but the lines and words and numbers are so interwoven that no one can really decode the locations they mark or their purpose. One of the women calls her over. She turns around and heads back to the table. She thinks she will ask the server about the map when they leave.

I want to take her hand and bring her back to the map. Tell her
it's o.k. that she doesn't understand. That she just needs to look—
closely, with patience.

I want to speak to her about cities spoken by women.

"The city of changes, constructed by memory and destroyed by
oblivion, is a city of death" (Tulli 2004).

"We are heirs and haunted, unknowingly. We are the descendants
of a body-city" (Cixous 2006).

"The theme of [city]-as-theatre: 'how to enter?', a theme with a
double stage and a double plot, one reflecting, relieving or sublating
translating the other: how to enter the desired city which can never
be found, always never there veiled commanded by a *fort da*? And
how to enter among the inhabitants of the city among whom one
is without being one finds oneself but crossed out, barred with bars
[*barré de barreaux*], struck through, thrown spat out.

"My theme: how to enter, how to *arrive* and *manage* [*arriver*] to
enter, how to get out of the outside in which one is locked up within
the inside?" (Cixous 2006).

The men and the woman at the next table are gone. She notices a sheet of glass covering their table. Pieces of paper with scribbled notes are tucked in the space between the glass and the tablecloth. She pauses to take a look. One of the women joins her and stares at the surface intently. She points to a large note right in the middle. She left it there a few months ago, the last time she was here. A man wrote the note for her.

It reads, "She is leaving. Why she is leaving, she doesn't even know herself. We tell her not to leave. She says O.K., but she still leaves. She leaves every time. She leaves only to return. She says this is the last time, definitely the last time; this time I am going to stay. But she leaves again and again. I ask her, What is out there? She says, Nothing. I ask her, What is here? She says, Everything. She leaves once again."

The note next to it reads, "Could one stay by leaving, leave by staying?" The one next to that reads, "What is the meaning of the café when its doors close at night, when there are no people in it, when no breath pollutes its air, when no eyes perceive its images?" The one next to that reads, "I want to know you, but I have left and you have arrived."

And underneath: "In order to read the map, you need a different language. To learn it . . ." and the rest is covered by another note, this one wordless and filled with coffee stains, invading the space

all the way to the table's edge. The woman puts a hand on

her shoulder. Their teas have arrived.

They join the rest of the group. She searches in her purse and puts

a blank piece of paper on the table. An invitation to pen something

while they sit around smoking, talking, drinking, sharing the halva,

murmuring prayers for the dead. They take turns writing.

"People who speak your language. Images that speak your city.

Black and white are dominant. But our lives are in color. Every day

a new color. The café should stay open so we can return."

"Some people you can't help but love. Like the old man who walks

back home, a cane in one hand, sangak bread in another. Like the

pharmacist who tells you the neighborhood women's favorite brands

of menstrual pads. Some places you can't help but love. Like the

cluttered old store around the corner, which sells everything and

nothing. Like the underground theater with its winding stairs and

small café. Like the gardens of a former palace turned museum.

Some places you can't help but remember, can't help but come

back to. No matter what, you have to return. One day. Some day."

"Loving. Talking. Nostalgia. Womanhood. Tea. Stories. Getting to

know a stranger. The café. This love. A cigarette."

"I want more of this."

"We hugged. You asked what was happening / and I didn't tell you
we were on death's program / but instead that we were going on
a journey, / one more, together, and that you shouldn't be afraid"
(Bolaño 2008).

corpse (15)
of the living
of the dead

Why do narratives of the dead cast a shadow over narratives of those who survived?

Why this obsession with stories of the dead?

Do we attend to these narratives of death because, frozen in a moment in time, they stop transforming and offer more manageable, straightforward stories than the constantly reconfiguring, ongoing stories of life?

Can narratives of death really be fixed when the very moment of death is perceived and remembered differently by different witnesses?

Does the finality of death imbue its narratives with meanings more symbolic than the narratives of life and of a people's attempts for survivance?

How does death define the experience of life?

"The earliest cities were cities of the dead. Among nomadic peoples the only fixed place was the tomb and the necropolis antedates the city of the living" (Jasper 2004).

Can the living even have a narrative without narratives of the dead?

How to constantly travel between the living and the dead? How to orchestrate the eternal relations between the two?

Why this obsession with the dead of one's time? With the history that unravels during one's time?

Are the events of one's present even considered history? When does the present become part of history?

Corpse (2)

Age: 22
Gender: Male
Occupation: University student
Date of Death: 10 Shahrivar 1390 / 1 September 2011
Place of Death: Tehran
Time of Death: Between 11:30 p.m. and 3:00 a.m.
Cause of Death: Suicide with pills
Date of Burial: 13 Shahrivar 1390 / 4 September 2011
Place of Burial: Behesht-e Javad al-Aemmeh, Mashhad

He and his two friends (a human-rights activist and a woman) are arrested at his house. Plainclothes agents. Forcing their way in. Taking them to Evin Prison.

The young woman is released a few days later. He, eight days later, on bail.

He is from Mashhad. Studies in Tehran. He is not a political activist. He is arrested because of his friendship with the activist. He is forced to provide false confessions against him.

According to some friends, he was a happy, funny guy before his arrest, with no previous signs of depression.

According to others, he had suffered severe depression for some time. He had thought of suicide and had spoken of it but never acted upon it.

Prison. Interrogation. Psychological torture. Threats. Humiliation.

Wardens. Cell mates.

Threats of being forced into false confessions.

After his release, his condition deteriorates. His family takes him to a psychiatrist. Plans are made for his admission to a clinic.

He commits suicide twenty-four days after his release.

The family last talks to him on the phone around midnight on Thursday. They find his lifeless body around three in the morning on Friday when they arrive at his house.

Police arrive. They disrespect the body and the family. The father and brother have to move the body by themselves, from their fourth-floor apartment to the ambulance.

Some believe the suicide was a result of the pressures of prison. Others mention his love for a woman, older than him, their relationship, the impossibility of their being together.

He was the youngest child. His parents came to Tehran from their hometown, Mashhad, to help with his release. Instead of him, they take home his corpse.

In accordance with his will, his organs are donated. The friend who is a human-rights activist leaves the country when ultimately released.

Why are some narratives retold until they become symbolic while others are never revisited?
What is the role of chance in stumbling over these narratives?
What qualities make one death more worthy of attention than another?
What if the cruelest deaths, the most violent, the most revealing of the techniques of the oppressor, are the ones that have yet to be disclosed?
What if they are yet to come?

She checks her phone to see if the sculptor has texted her. He told her he would let her know if he was able to find time this evening for a meeting. Nothing. It's time to go home. The women decide they should put the paper with their notes next to the others. They tuck it on the left side. A memory.

It's as if they want to leave behind a trace, proof that it happened.
This togetherness. This drinking tea. Just being. Here. It's as if
they want to hold on to the memory. But the notes are not really
the memory. They are texts born of the memory. Its representation.
Within them there is an urge to turn this moment into the past
and flee it, but there is also the urge to return to it, discover it,
rediscover it.

They say Iranians are a nostalgic people. We wonder why memories
follow us from the past into the present and further, why we insist
on carrying them. Perhaps we fear that if we release them from
ourselves, they might stop being true. Maybe we need to learn
to create memories of the future too. Learn to remember things
before they even happen. Learn to be nostalgic for the future.
Perhaps we are no more nostalgic than others but have come to
develop a sense of urgency for personal archiving, for embodying
the past. In the absence of official archives, in the presence, even,
of systematized erasure of the past, the body and the unconscious
become depositories for archives, hidden, dormant, lying in wait.
But what about archiving systematically, consciously? How to move
toward it? How to encompass a time and a place in an archive that
extends beyond the bodies of its people?

How to encompass the infinite on the page, between the covers of
a book?

Will the archive ever be whole when we do not have access to the
voices of the dead? To their thoughts and minds in the moments
before death?

What is an archive when it cannot hold on to all that a moment is in
the middle of a protest, the moment when someone throws tear gas
and someone shouts and someone tastes the bitterness of the air on
her tongue, when someone touches the arm of a stranger and pulls
him into an alley, when someone hears a gunshot but doesn't know

what it is or where it has come from, the moment when everything goes black, the moment when everything becomes silent?

What is an archive when it cannot hold on to all that a moment is in the middle of the stillness of solitary confinement?

What is an archive when it cannot hold on to any moment in its totality?

What is an archive of an era, of a people?

How should the archive be compiled? How should the archive be organized?

What will the archive teach us?

She looks for the note about the map and the language among the older scraps of paper. She looks for it and cannot find it. She finds the middle one, once again follows the trail her eyes followed earlier. She finds the second and third and fourth and fifth notes, a chain of paper and words that runs to the coffee-covered scrap at the edge of the table, but there is no trace of the note about the map and the language. She wants to remove the glass top and search for it. The women call for her as they go down the stairs. The server arrives at the table with a new group. She takes one last look and walks away.

The red pins on the map are all gone. She also notices an old sliding blade with a wooden frame suspended over the staircase. It looks as if it has been lifted from a guillotine. She hadn't seen it on the way up. Downstairs, in the hallway that leads to the café door, stands an old telephone booth with the glass panes removed. The old machine is missing a few keys and looks scratched as if by coins and pens and knives. Old newspapers wallpaper the upper part of the café's cement walls. The women have already paid and are waiting outside. On the sidewalk, a kitten is meowing for her food. She asks the man standing behind the counter about the red pins on the map. Without even looking up from the cucumber-mint sekanjabin he's mixing, he says, What pins? Take a look at our store sign. Have a wonderful night.

Stepping out, she crouches to pet the kitten and looks up at the sign: "KaféKa," spelled out in wood with red pins. She wants to go back in and check the upstairs map again, but the door to the café is closed, the curtains are already drawn, and the lights are turning off inside, one after another.

corpse (19)
missing links

How to bear the void?

How to bear loss? On one's skin, on one's hair, on one's lashes, on one's nails, on one's nerves, on one's cells, in one's heart, on one's tongue?

How to translate loss into language?

How to survive loss?

What is at the center of loss? At the center of life after loss?

How much time needs to pass before mourning can become healing can become living?

How can we walk the distance that separates you and me, you and us, who became one and the Other because a shared experience exploded into an abyss of unshared history, memory, story?

How can we walk the distance and arrive on the other side, alive and generous, capable of light and love, reaching in and reaching out with a touch and a tone that can make joy and be joy?

Are we, as we walk, leaving the dead behind?

Are we leaving ourselves behind?

What about guilt?

What about shame?

Mine and yours?

Ours and yours?

How to bear memory?

How to bear witness?

And what about witnessing, remembering, documenting, and archiving dreams? How to embrace and represent the endlessness of dreams? How to word the world of the unconscious and the subconscious? Defined by its very own rules. Defying all perimeters of storytelling and meaning-making. Accessible only through forever-imperfect interpretations/translations. As yet indecipherable.

The moon is full, and on the terrace she has spread the white-and-pink floral cushions on the black metal chairs and a few cushions of rough, nomadic-style fabric on the stone floor. The moon is full up there in the sky, and the light of the few stars has faded in the face of its light, and some have filled their glasses with vodka and fruit juice, and some have brought the wine bottles and their glasses and plates and bowls of mezes outside to the table, which is covered by a tablecloth that was once the fresh green of grass but, after weeks left out under the blazing sun and in the dust from construction sites nearby, has faded to the green of the pistachios in the bowl of mixed nuts, and yet it has kept its dark-blue dots, dots that are the color of the dark blue of the city night, the city on less polluted nights, on nights like tonight. The moon is full up there in the sky, and the tall metallic crane has fixed its leg in the earth of the huge pit where the once-upon-a-time villa stood, off the main alley to the right of the building, and the crane has risen high, has reached its arm out to touch the round face of the lover moon that is sitting up there in the sky all naked and stretched out, while the trees and the lights and the dust and the air and the noise of the city swoon over the songs from the iPod in the living room coming through the wide-open French doors to where they all are now settling. "I feel

I know you / I don't know how / I don't know why . . ." "We spent some time doing one thing or another / Never really mattered as long as we were together . . ." "My home has no heart / My home has no veins / If you try to break in / It bleeds with no stains . . ." "T'as pas le droit d'avoir moins mal que moi / Si j'ai mal, c'est pas normal que toi, tu n'aies pas mal . . ." "Everybody wants to rule the world / It's my own design / It's my own remorse . . ." The moon is full up there in the sky, shining a frame around their togetherness with one another and with the plants, with the metal chairs and the table covered with glasses, small bowls of cherries and chips and cucumber-yogurt dip and nuts, an ashtray shaped like a cockroach, a tiny candleholder, and two iPhones. The cat appears out of nowhere, appears whenever it wishes, coming to this house to be fed, to lie on her couch, to interrupt the movement of her fingers on the laptop, to be caressed by those very fingers. The cat appears through the bamboo that lines the short terrace wall, and a light goes off in a window of the villa overlooking the courtyard and terrace only to go on in another window, and the cat swishes past the legs of the woman who calls to it lovingly and the legs of the woman who fears animals and the legs of the man sipping his vodka nonchalantly and the legs of the man discussing the latest art auction and the legs of the woman listening closely to him, finally finding there the familiar scent it is looking for and curling up with a purr on her lap, on the cushions on the floor, and letting its neck be stroked.

The moon is full, and the man, whom she doesn't know, who has

come with a friend, whom she knows is a wonderful artist but

who is so full of himself, heatedly discusses the auctions and the

pieces and the prices, the hands behind the scenes and the money

laundering, the fake exports and the fake artworks, the figures and

the names and the mix of colors and the strokes of brushes, the

image of a nightmare, the room with a view of Dali's surrealism,

the shades of a woman's intestines, the broken engine of an old

Beetle, the souls' shadows, the sewn eyes, the shattered statues,

the face of the sun on an ochre wall, the coins tossed in a tar case

on some Mediterranean sidewalk, black ink afloat on white paper,

disrupting and concealing the image of the nightmare.

The moon is full, and the woman listens carefully, trying to

memorize his words, the names and the banknotes, thinking she

needs to ask the friend who has brought this man to arrange a

meeting so they can talk art and statues, pretending she is listening

not to him but to the water rising from the small fountain in

another corner of the terrace, looking at the cat's eyes and the

hands and fingers and shoes and legs of the men and women

all around and the light spilling over the terrace from inside the

apartment. She smooths the white dress floating around her body

and runs a hand through her short black hair and stares at the

watch on the wrist of the man she has been desiring, the hand

holding a digital camera, the fingers changing the settings, the eyes hidden behind the lens through which he's looking at the moon, the moon high up there in the sky looking down on them. The light of the upstairs neighbor goes off, and the playlist comes to an end, and she hands the cat to the woman next to her, and she gets up and takes a few dirty plates and an empty bowl and her glass of wine to the kitchen.

She cleans up a bit, brews tea for later, puts together a tray of sweets and fruits, and prepares to go back outside. At the threshold, she almost bumps into him as he comes inside to put down his camera and go to the bathroom, and she takes in the scent of his cologne, and he asks her if she needs help, and she tastes the weight of her own breath and hears the muscles of his body, and the second is only a second but it's longer than a second, and she says he can take the sweets and fruits outside, and he gives her his camera, and she sends him out again. She goes to the bathroom to pee but forgets and instead splashes water on her face and puts on more red lipstick, and, before heading back to the terrace, she chooses another playlist and turns the volume down a bit and takes the poetry book from the shelf and her wine glass from the kitchen counter and walks out under the moon, so full up there in the night sky, slowly moving farther and farther away from the crane.

If, in the city, "the established symbolic order is the 'Law of the Father,' and it is discovered to be not only repressive but false, distorted by the *illogicality* of bias, then the new symbolic order is to be a 'woman's language,' corresponding to a woman's desire" (Hejinian 2009).

A woman's language. Spiral. Sprawling. Moving in and out. Meandering toward and away. Breathing in and breathing out. As if a jellyfish expanding and contracting to move its body forward through rough water.

A woman's language, like a woman's body. A woman's language, like a woman's desire. Opening to embrace and nurture an Other in its womb and thereafter. Closing only to hold on to and defend an Other or the self against the bodies of intruders. Exploding into formation within a constellation of past, present, and future female (hi)stories, which the official, rigid, patriarchal narrative intends to erase and forget. Weaving its definition with threads of a female lineage that the power-hungry, male-dominated hierarchy hopes to undermine and disrupt.

A woman's language speaking the narrative of a city that does not abide or end, a language embracing openness, attempting to continually redefine its openness.

She gives the book to the woman petting the cat, who hands the cat
to the man sliding a cigarette from a pack, who holds the cat only
for a second then puts it down on the floor to light his cigarette.
The cat meows and walks quietly toward the bamboo to hide in its
shadow. She fills her glass and swallows half the wine as she sits
down again on the cushions on the floor, feeling the moon fulling
and her body fooling around, wanting the man she wants to follow
her bare feet, her ankles, and what of her legs he can see at the
hem of her dress, wanting him to take in her scent, see the corner
of her mouth curving into a smile as she takes a stealthy look at
his lips, his beard, his neck, wanting the artist and whomever he's
talking with to shut up, wanting the woman to whom she handed
the book of poetry to open it and read a poem for divination, for the
metal wings of the butterflies resting on the metal vines erected in
the jasmine pot, for the tiny feet of the ceramic lizards and turtles
strolling among the pots of geraniums, peonies, and rosemary, to
read a poem for divination, for the gestures of the night, for light,
for flesh, for breath. She hushes everyone and asks them to say the
prayer and asks her to open the book, and she sips the rest of the
wine and waits for the poem, feeling the touch of his gaze on her
fingers around the wine glass. She reads the poem, and the moon

reaches for the peak of the blue darkness of the sky, for its highness, for its vastness, reaches for the life, for the life and death in their bodies down below, and the cat jumps sleepily over the wall behind the bamboo and wanders into the alley toward the neighbor's house, the house she calls home, as they begin to repeat the final line of the poem.

They drink freshly brewed tea, some discussing the poem and others not caring, until some get up to help clean off the table, and they all head inside, and the playlist has long since ended. They invade the living room's silence with their voices, moving from the outside that is the terrace to the inside that is the apartment and soon to the outside that is the alley then into their cars, toward their homes. Hope-to-see-you-soons and promises for another gathering take only as long as it takes to grab the keys, to cover up with manteaus and scarves, to put kisses on cheeks, and when the friend and the artist so full of himself step toward her to say good-night, she rushes to ask the artist if they can meet to discuss the auctions and artworks, but he says he is going abroad in two days for a show and vacation, he's sorry but he's too busy until then, and she wants to push him to make this happen, but the body of the man she wants badly tonight comes closer to hers in a frame of late-night wine and tea breath, and he embraces her and says he hopes to see her soon, and she forgets about the artist leaving for a show and vacation and the friend who brought him, and the two

are out the door in no time, and she wonders whether she should
ask the man she wants tonight to stay, but she doesn't find the
right words, and then he too leaves with another friend, who is
giving him a ride back home.
And a second is not just a second, and fifteen minutes is the time it
takes her to empty the bowls and organize what is left of the food
in the fridge and put the plates and glasses in the sink and bring
the cushions in and turn off the lights and lie down on the couch
and light a cigarette in the light of the moon, whose round body is
not in the frame of any glass panes anymore but whose light is still
seeping into the living room, spreading its warmth over the lion
and the gazelles and the birds of the hand-woven carpet that covers
a patch of the stone floor. And fifteen minutes is the time it takes
her to realize she cannot wait for him and for the soon he spoke of.
She picks up her phone and texts him and asks whether now is
soon enough, gets a text back immediately that says it is already
beyond soon, that says he shouldn't have left, that says he should've
kissed her before leaving, that says he'll make up for it, that asks
how should he make up for it, and she texts him back and says what
about trying to make up for it now, gets a text back that says now
is the time to try to make up for it, that says he's just gotten home
but that he'll call a cab and be on his way, don't fall asleep and I'll
be there soon, and she texts him back and says she'll be waiting.
And fifteen minutes double is the time it takes him to call a cab and

wait for it and ride again through the very same streets only now in the reverse direction, for her to wait for him on the couch with another cigarette and another, telling herself she needs to write down what the artist was saying, the names, the titles, the prices, before she forgets, but instead she rolls a joint, and her index finger fumbles with her phone's keypad, and she rereads his messages and gets new ones that say he'll be there in ten minutes, in five minutes, in two minutes, can't wait to get there. She goes to the bathroom and freshens up and opens the French doors, all of them wide open once again. And after fifteen minutes double plus a few more, the lobby man buzzes her to let her know, in a sleepy voice filled with disapproving question marks he tries to hide, that she has a guest, and she opens the apartment door to him.

Corpse (3)

Age: 37
Gender: Female
Occupation: Manager at a company, university student majoring in law
Date of Death: 7 Mehr 1390 / 29 September 2011
Place of Death: Tehran
Time of Death: Morning, exact time unknown
Cause of Death: Suicide with pills
Date of Burial: Exact date unknown, a few days after death
Place of Burial: Behesht-e Zahra Cemetery, Tehran

Rumors of her arrest. Along with her beloved and their mutual friend, a human-rights activist. The rumors are later denied. She was not arrested. The two men were. Along with another friend.

Those who speak of her arrest speak of the psychological pressure of interrogation, of her being threatened, of her being forced into false confessions on TV, of her fear. Her beloved commits suicide twenty-four days after his release.

She, almost a month after that. On a Thursday. The day of their trysts.

Some condemn the speculation that the suicide had political motives. Others deny that it had to do with love.

The father speaks. He denies her relationship with the young man. Not love. Not lovers. Just friendship, he says. A short while, he says.

On her blog, she writes of the man. Of their love and of their longings.

The father says he does not want to deny the words on her blog, he wants to deny the rumors.

His voice trembles. He cries.

He speaks of her spirits, emotional and fragile. Of her listening to and being pained by the pain of others, by the conditions of society. Of her studying and working. Of her friends calling her "Mom." Of her visiting the elderly. Of her supporting orphans. Of her feeling that she did not belong. Of her telling him she felt exhausted.

He calls her and her suicide nonpolitical. Calls the timing of the two suicides a coincidence. Says she had grown so sensitive that her suicide could have been prompted by the news of any other's suicide.

He denies her arrest.

His voice trembles. He cries.

He speaks of him and her mother being at work that morning, of her colleagues calling an hour later to say she had not shown up to work, of her mother returning home, hearing calming music, finding her body, the message on the mirror:

"No wailing.

No crying.

I will be eternal.

I love you all."

In her last blog post, a week before her suicide, she writes of her beloved:

"I swear to our Thursdays . . .

Today is Thursday.

Come my love,

Let's dance

On Thursdays . . ."

Many posts are addressed to him.

Whispers of love, for love.

Of him, for him.

She calls him, she misses him, she aches for him.

"I am done," she writes at the end of the post before the last. The post is written in red ink.

A YouTube link to an Astor Piazzolla tango called "Oblivion." A YouTube link to a black-and-white video of an orchestra performing an Eleni Karaindrou composition. Several YouTube links to videos not available anymore.

Her blog is still alive. Up in the virtual world. Visited and quoted more than ever immediately after the suicide.

The ceremonies of the seventh and fortieth nights following her death are held in private.

A UK article calls them the modern-day Romeo and Juliet. A blog suggests commemorating the day of her suicide, the seventh day of the seventh month of the Persian calendar, as the new St. Valentine's Day in Iran.

And she grabs him, and he grabs her, and he pulls her toward

him impatiently but gently and puts his mouth over hers, and she

throws her arms around him and moves her fingers through his

hair and his beard, and their tongues meet in the vortex of the front

hallway, and they begin shedding their clothes as they feel their

way to the bedroom while clinging to each other. It all takes only a

second, but it's a second that will forever be their first, a second that

is not just a second but is a second and a breath, a breath, a giggle,

a breath, a breath, a sigh, another breath, and the sound of phones

falling to the floor next to her bed, and another breath, and another

breath, and a pause as she throws the bedcover to one side and the

two of them, now completely naked, get into bed. He touches her

wetness and asks in a whisper, what shall we do with these bodies?

and she takes his hand and guides him inside her as the moon

continues to grow a bit more full or a bit less full, fooling around in

its universe while watching over the fools the two of them are.

Why should we tell the story of the dead? Why should we research these deaths? Why should we resurrect the dead? Should we? Can we?

Are the dead really gone? Are the dead more present than the living, their ghosts forever hovering, casting shadows, haunting the living responsible for or indifferent to or helpless against their displacement?

If these deaths have already been researched and documented, why another documentation? If the stories of these bodies have already been told, why tell them again? What is it about translating them anew? What is it about relating to them anew? What is the raison d'être for these narratives? What is their use?

Is the new context important? The voice? The style?

Will retelling them in the form of art, in the body of a story, change the meaning, the transferring, the impact?

Why these men and women? Why not others? How many were they—those killed during or after the 2009 protests? What about the counted and uncounted dead killed during the 1980s? Why not the ones assassinated during the Chain murders in 1998 and earlier—writers, translators, poets, activists? Why not their stories? Why not their stories too?

What about others? Were there others? Who were the others, before them, after them?

Re: the dream world.

"Dreams yield no more than *fragments* of reproductions" of
experiences; they include only "loosely associated elements"; they
are "lacking in intelligibility and orderliness" (Freud 2010).
Thinking "predominantly in visual images" (Freud 2010), they
enjoy "plasticity" and "symbolic multiplicity" (Notley 2014).
They are "a glimpse of something incognito" (Carson 2006).
I do not speak the language of dreams, but I will not turn away
from their story, their world.
The dream world gains materiality out of the documentation of
my dreams, from December 2011 to January 2014. The dreams
are documented either in Persian or English, whichever language
imposes itself on my body and the page. The dreams are dreamt in
different cities around the world but mainly in Tehran and Denver.

corpse (23)
the government accepts
responsibility
for only a few of the corpses

The rain, they say, cleanses the city of soot, makes the air clean and fresh, but that only happens later, later when the rain has stopped, and even then the freshness in the air lasts only a few hours until the cars join forces on the ground to pollute the air once again, to remind us all of their powers, of the battle between the down below and the up above. And down below in the city, wet, they are, and muddy: the alleys, the highways, the gutters, the sewage channels. A hassle, they are: to walk through, to jump over, to smell or try not to smell. And the patches of green and flowerbeds on the corners or along the highways, a joy, they are: to glance at, to breathe in, to walk past. All the while, she meanders between the cars, the buses, the motorbikes, the vans, the cars, the flower boys, the flower girls, the newspaper woman, the CD man, the cars, the pedestrians, the ambulance stuck in traffic, the traffic, which is a knot of metal and human bodies suspended in the countdown for a red light, and they count again and again and no space opens up for the cars or the ambulance, the ambulance, the ambulance. Is the person inside already dead or still alive? Is the person inside, who is alive, going to die in traffic or in the hospital? Isn't the person staying alive going to die anyway, someday, somewhere? The rain pours down and washes the soot away.

Wet, she is, even though she carries an umbrella. Wet, she is, when she gets to the bus stop and waits for the bus, which opens its doors to her and the other passengers before even arriving at the stop and closes its doors and keeps on moving since everyone has already boarded before the stop, and the stop is empty, and the bus is not going to break for the no one who remains at the stop.

She stands in the not-yet-crowded aisle and lets a large group of women and kids coming through the back door take the few remaining seats and lets herself forget about the outside of the inside of this moving theater.

The women and kids are not from the north of the city; she can tell from the way they wear their veils and the way they carry themselves and their bags. The women and kids have traveled to the north of the city, perhaps to pay a visit to the mausoleum, because it is Wednesday, and the buried saint is more responsive to prayers, they say, on Wednesdays, especially on the last Wednesday of the month. It is the last Wednesday of the month. The women and kids have paid a visit to the mausoleum that is tucked in the heart of the bazaar, have given the vendor at the corner of the courtyard some banknotes in exchange for bags of wheat and millet to throw for the pigeons of the mausoleum, have said a prayer or two and cried a little or a lot, have knotted a piece of cloth from an old flowery sheet or veil to the bars of the gold shrine in hopes that their prayers will be answered, and then they've headed back out to the bazaar. The women and kids scurry from one store to another, buy some walnuts or a small bag of fresh peppers or jars of homemade pickled vegetables, not because they don't know how to pickle things at home or they don't have time for it or they don't do it, but perhaps for the pleasure of buying rather than toiling in the kitchen, or perhaps so they can taste them with the family and brag to themselves and to the husbands and the kids that their own pickles taste much better, that these ones were just a waste of money, and they glow inside with the joy of this realization and the joy of hearing the husbands and kids finally confess that of course there are none as good as theirs, and they buy a new set of tea glasses or some heavy-duty trash bags or new prayer beads or old-style bars of cedar soap or lace underwear from a women-only shop or tobacco for the hookah after minutes and minutes of bargaining with the salesperson, or perhaps they leave without buying anything because they did not agree with the salesperson's final offer, leave only to stop before a street vendor and buy a plastic made-in-China tablecloth or a grater or a book of prayers or boxes of matches or a pack of six black socks for the husband or a skirt that they do not really need but buy simply because it is cheap, cheaper than the price a store would offer, because the vendor is a bargainer like the women, who enjoy the bargaining as much as or more than the purchase itself, the object they have needed or desired or not, which they now carry with them in plastic bags onto the bus.

What kinds of mausoleums are erected for today's dead? For those celebrated by the regime? Those effaced by the regime?
Could archives in the digital realm be the mausoleums of today and tomorrow? Will they survive long enough? Will they survive at all?

The women and kids who are now the women and kids with bags
filled with this and that settle in their seats, and the fat woman
wearing a colorful veil sits down in a window seat and leaves a
big plastic bag with several other bags inside it on the seat next to
her, and the woman wearing a black veil, whose features are not
dissimilar to the other's but who is younger, finds a place across
the aisle from her. They sit the kids down in the row in front of
the woman in the black veil, and the kids instantly forget about
everyone and everything around them apart from the Cheetos
bag they are passing around and their soccer trading cards. The
younger woman immediately takes out her cell phone and begins
dialing and talking so loudly that not only the women around her
but also the men in the front section and perhaps the driver, too,
can hear, and while the men resume their own after-a-long-day-let's-
complain-about-the-hardships-of-life conversations a minute later,
the women all keep silent or continue in lower voices and listen, or
hear anyway, as the woman tells the listener on the other end of the
line that tonight they should go with their families to visit a couple
just back from a trip, discussing whether to buy the couple a gift
or sweets and flowers, adding that they'll figure that out when the
woman on the bus gets home and calls the woman on the phone

back again, in an hour or two, and as the woman in black says good-bye to the woman on the other end of the line, the women on the bus all echo the regards she sends to the beloved husband of the woman on the other end of the line, the kiss for the little devils at home. The woman sitting in the row behind the woman in the colorful veil smiles at this conversation, and her eyes and the eyes of the woman still standing in the aisle meet, and they smile at one another, and the woman in the colorful veil, as if she has only now become aware of the one still standing, begins to move her bags onto her lap and tells the one standing, come sit, my daughter, and finally, the one standing does. The woman in the colorful veil talks over her to the woman in the black veil, who is not on the phone anymore, who, in response to the woman's question about the phone call, tells them all about the couple who has returned from Karbala, to whom they must pay a visit, oh, pay a visit after this long day, oh, in this rain, which doesn't seem to want to stop anytime soon, oh, get everyone ready and going. Suddenly she pauses and looks out, leaving the story unfinished, and asks, as if she has just remembered, about the stop where she needs to get off, asks how far away they are, how many stops, and when she is assured that she still has some time to travel on the moving stage, she calls out to her young boys, whose fingers are all orange from the Cheetos and who are swapping cards with one another, to sit together in one seat so the middle-aged woman who has just boarded can sit down,

do, please, sit down, kids, come on, hurry up, move, move, make
some room for the lady, and then the woman in the black veil moves
to a window seat that has just opened up, and a college student
who carries a laptop, backpack, and folder takes her seat, not even
looking up from her texts for a second. When the bus driver calls
out, over all the mumbling and chattering, the name of the stop the
woman in black has asked for, she gets up and summons the boys,
hurry, hurry, boys, get your things, let's go, get going, walk, hurry
up, shouting to the driver over the bodies of the men, don't move
yet, we haven't gotten off, then taking her time in putting a kiss on
the cheek of the woman in the colorful veil, who, it turns out, is her
mother, the way she addresses her, tells her to take care, to take her
medication on time, and not to forget to get off at the stop where
she needs to get off, asks the woman sitting next to her mother, can
you please make sure she gets off at the right stop? I appreciate it,
may beautiful God grant all your wishes, and as she begins to move
away toward the door, the woman still sitting behind the mother
asks her to send everyone's regards to the couple who has returned
from pilgrimage, and the woman in the black veil and the woman
in the colorful veil smile such carefree smiles that she, now sitting
next to the mother, wonders where that comes from and how they
nourish it, but she doesn't want to ask and be given a sermon about
faith and family, ask and be asked questions in turn: Is she married
or not, does she have kids or not, does she study or not?

"the trickster is informer is infernal pass it on / the nomad leaves tracks / today came all the way inside / the prognosticator left some assonance / we are tangential are instrumental / my guts spilled out as testament / to the best & worst in women" (Waldman 1976). A women-only space. Such spaces are often spoken of only in terms of the oppression and victimhood they inflict upon their inhabitants. But spaces of separation can also be sites for building connections, for reaching out, for reaching in, for seeing anew, for redefining, not just the self but also the collective.
How to shift the perspective and adjust the self toward the Other to imagine a new "we"?
To begin, one needs to "identify marginality as much more than a site of deprivation," as "a site of radical possibility, a space of resistance." Marginality is "a central location for the production of a counter-hegemonic discourse that is not just found in words but in habits of being and the way one lives" (hooks 1990).

Instead, she wants to shout out, ask the daughter in the black veil

not to leave, please stay on for just a few more stops, let's get

off together at the square where I'm headed, where you should be

headed, where all of us, women and men, should be headed, to the

square where there once was a statue of a mother who grew fresh

narcissus in her heart, for lovers to pluck while they held candles

during vigils, a mother who kept growing the flowers so lovers

could keep plucking them, a mother who, amid the city smog,

breastfed the child she held in her arms with the scent of narcissus,

whispering to her, the secrets are with the mothers, the mothers

and the lovers, telling her the stories of each and every petal, the

square where now, there is only the void of the mother and the

child and her narcissus, the void into whose nothingness lovers

stealthily stare, with candles or without candles, pausing only for a

moment before continuing on their way, not even turning to look

back, not knowing where to search, who to ask, how to find.

She wants to tell her, tell them, wants to hear herself speak

about the statue that disappeared. The mother. The child. The

narcissus in her heart, in her flesh. The lovers. No footprints or

fingerprints left behind. No signs of who or how or when or why.

She wants to speak of the statue that disappeared after being threatened for months. Of ropes found around her neck, tied as if to execute her. Of the ropes that remained hanging. For a few days. Until they removed them. Cleaned the mother and the child. Made them shine. She wants to hear herself speak about the narcissus shattering in the statue's heart, the flowers beginning to wither. For a few days. Until some lovers removed the dead ones. Tended to the rest. About the mother who stayed standing. Holding on to her child. Giving birth to narcissus. For a while. Until she was not. Until she disappeared. Taking the child and the flowers with her. Leaving behind some narcissus petals that also disappeared shortly after, swept away by a gust of wind or the dustman or the lovers who arrived in time to collect them as souvenirs.

In an interview on March 11, 2010, Zahra Rahnavard, wife of the
Green Movement leader Mir-Hossein Mousavi, is asked about the
vandalism of one of her "most famous pieces," "one of the most
famous sculptures in Iran during the first two decades of the Islamic
Republic" (Rahnavard 2011). The statue is of a woman. Ropes have
been put around the woman's neck. As if she is to be hanged. The
woman is a mother. The statue is called *Mother*. The square in
Tehran where the piece is located is called Mother Square.
Rahnavard responds, "For artists, their work is as close to them
as their body. It comes from the heart. The artist puts all of his or
her love into art, and it becomes the tale of all the untold stories,
cries, secrets, morals, and dreams that the artist has. But when
the extremist forces are taking people's lives just because they seek
freedom, whether it is through executions, brutal beatings or other
means, what can we expect them to do with a bronze statue? How
can they understand what this statue stands for? How can they
understand motherhood and art?" (Rahnavard 2011).
Mother is later draped in cloth for some time, under the pretext
of being restored. It, however, never went missing. The mother
and child statue that actually went missing, in spring of 2010,
was another, by another artist, located in another public square
in Tehran. The two artworks and their nonfictional fates blur in
the fictional realm. The two bodies become related and translate
into one.
Rahnavard and Mousavi were put under house arrest in February
2011. In February 2019, they are still under house arrest. No trial
has been held.

She wants to shout out to the woman in the black veil, wants to ask
her to stay, ask them all to stay, wonders if the bus driver would
take them there so they could get off together and circle the square
and stare into the void, stare into the void together, together, but
the woman in the black veil is already gone, and the bus is already
back in traffic, and the mother in the colorful veil sitting next to her
is busy rummaging through her bags, examining the souvenirs
from her trip to the mausoleum.

What are the facts of the void inherited? What are its fictions? How much of what is deemed fact is fiction? How much of fiction is fact? When an event has come to an end and only reverberations remain, can a hard line really be drawn between the two?

What do mausoleums pay homage to? The facts or the fictions of dead figures? What kinds of memories do they conjure? What kinds of stories do they tell?

What is the nature of memory? What does it do to us?

What is the use of memory in the larger context of history?

What is the use of stories in the larger context of politics?

What parts of memory are collective? What parts are private?

What is the use of looking back? What kind of looking back is useful? For the present? For the future?

What is the use of looking to the dead?

How different are mausoleums and monuments? What different functions do they play in relation to the dead? To the living?

How do their eras and contexts define their roles?

How do their different relations with public space affect our relations with them and with the space?

Do we engage more emotionally with one and more intellectually with the other?

Why has one become more associated with religion than the other?

How does the presence of a tomb in one and its absence in the other affect our relations with them and with what they commemorate?

How differently do they affect our readings of the dead, of the past? Our continuous writing of them?

Why do we create idols of the dead? Why do we need them as symbols, as markers of time and place?

How do different generations look back at the revered dead of a particular era?

How does the passage of time and a change of context redefine their meanings and our relations with them?

corpse (33)
the blame is always elsewhere

She needs to see the sculptor. She hopes he can provide her with some answers. She asks a friend who knows him to take her to him. She knows he has wanted to sculpt the friend's body for some time. She hopes he, with his connections, might lead her to clues about the missing statues, although none of them are his. The two women arrive. One rings the bell. The door remains shut for a while. Cars pass. Cars brake for a second. The scent of kebab from a nearby restaurant mingles with the motor oil on the floor of an auto shop, mingles with the water cleansing windshields and tires in a car wash, mingles with the smoke coming out of exhaust pipes, with the scent of coffee from a café, with the sounds of iron beams being laid on the thirteenth floor of a building nearby, with the gaze of onlookers staring at recycled neon signs on a gallery wall that call for revolution, at the weight of chicken legs in glass cases, at the feet and mouths of kids running around, at the metal of another door just around the corner closed to everyone but its owners. The door in front of them remains closed, too, but only for one more second, and then it opens. The hinges make a noise as if the door has not opened for years, or it has opened, but whoever opened it didn't mind the noise, or they minded, but decided the noise should remain as a signal that the outside is flowing in, and one needs to keep the door shut

or shut it as quickly as possible.

She almost stumbles on the threshold as the door opens to them.

Beyond is a garden that spreads as far as the eye can see, and

she freezes right there on the threshold, as if this place is the

culmination of all times that once were and are to come, as if this

time is the concentration of all places around the city and beyond,

as if nonexistence grows its roots into the soil of this here and now

that is neither outside nor inside, giving life to an existence that

speaks its own language, a language not understood by everyone,

and even those who think they understand it may only be under the

illusion that they do, and those who think they don't understand

it actually may. She closes the door and steps in behind the friend.

To the left, an adobe building sits silently. The friend tells her

it's a library. The friend walks on. She pauses. There is a lock on

the door. Rusted. The windows are covered with old newspapers

shaded with the residue of water that may have been meant for the

flowers and trees, water not meant for the trees turned window

coverings, turned collages, canvases, or papier-mâché bodies stored

behind closed doors. The path winds, and the friend walks, and

she follows behind making a list of all the things she needs to pay

attention to or needs to ask, but only discreetly, because she doesn't

want anyone to know that she's looking for the bronze bodies, the

nonmoving bronze bodies that were publicly exposed to the private bodies of flesh and blood moving throughout the city, bronze bodies that had to stand still where they landed so that the city could mean its meaning, bronze bodies that, once stolen and moved, were, with their absence and silence, trying to signal failures of the city and its bodies and its meanings.

"Monuments are destroyed, altered or vandalized for a variety of reasons related to the meanings they have. One reason is certainly to demonstrate one's opposition to what the work represents beyond its literal depiction of a person . . . Indeed, having this kind of effigy on which to enact opposition and to demonstrate that opposition to the world in a very visible fashion is a clear advantage of the presence of such works in public space. . . . People also deform or destroy a monument to demonstrate their opposition not to its subject matter—that is to the people, cause or belief it represents—but to the *manner* in which it does so" (Franck 2015). Monuments may also be vandalized for reasons that have nothing to do with their subject matter or the manner in which they present it. They may be vandalized to demonstrate opposition to any one of the elements at work in the system that has given the monuments a presence in time and space. They may become sites of conflict not just between the people and the authorities in charge of the monuments, but also between the various factions of a regime keeping an eye on the spaces the monuments inhabit. They may become bodies used as tools for negotiation. Or they may simply be vandalized or stolen because the material they are built from has, for the vandals, monetary value far greater than their aesthetic, social, or historical value.

And so she goes looking, searching without asking, sifting through whatever the city and its bodies reveal, not wanting to excavate or exhume, not wanting to make a noise or draw attention to herself, hoping to slink quietly toward the lost bodies and resurrect them.

I sometimes wish that she weren't so discreet, that she would take risks, even act carelessly, simply aim for the heart of the matter rather than tiptoe on the periphery. But it is not that easy, I know. And I ask (her, myself) whether anything can be accomplished without taking risks, without making noise, without drawing attention. But I can also understand her hesitations.

If the search for the truths and their telling bring the seeker and the speaker to exile or to imprisonment, isn't that one more voice silenced, one more dead body added to the list?

How far can she go before being silenced?

Is silence the death of the storyteller?

Or does the storyteller die only in physical death?

Does the storyteller ever really die?

How should one tell stories in the face of death?

Does the shadow of death that hangs over us haunt us or guide us?

The friend walks, and she follows. Dogs begin to bark. She stops where she is and looks around, hearing their voices, not seeing their faces. The friend turns and mumbles something reassuring, but it's lost in the barking, and then they hear the words of the sculptor rising above, silencing the barking, and only then do they continue on the path, which meanders along the brick walls, which didn't always exist but now run behind the bushes along the highway, which didn't always exist but now does along the path that winds through the garden, which is not harnessed but is watered, which is not symmetrical or asymmetrical but haphazardly organized, and they walk until they arrive at an entryway with two benches along the walls, and underneath and over them dozens of baskets of fruit from the garden, persimmons and oranges and tangerines and shelled walnuts, and there, at the end, they reach another door and the man, the sculptor, the painter, who waits for them at the threshold. Beyond the threshold, the two women sit, and he offers them tea or coffee, and they both ask for tea, and he walks to the kitchen, and she notices the sparkle in his eyes when he casts the friend a glance, a glance that is a gaze, a gaze following the contours of her body, the body she knows he desires to form from marble or bronze or adobe, the body she knows he admires as the body of a Greek or Roman goddess, the body she knows he wants to see naked but has not yet, the body she knows he has already begun to draw, the face, the neck, the shoulders, not yet the rest, with the touch of his gaze, not the touch of his fingers, not the touch of skin to skin, of fingers to belly, of fingernails to knees, of fingertips to inner thighs, but drawing nonetheless, waiting, waiting patiently, waiting hopefully. He waits for the friend to shed her clothes and sit there on the stool then move the stool aside and lie down on the white sheet covering the paint-splashed gabbeh. He waits for the friend to unveil herself to him so he can make of her a memorial to the seduction and enigma embodied in her green eyes, which, though they won't be green in the statue, will still seduce and mystify: absorbing, devouring, asking, demanding, winding, unwinding. Or he waits for the friend to say, no, I can't do this, no, I don't want to do this, so he can hold her hands in his one last time and say his good-bye as she walks away from him through the entryway and onto the path toward the rusted door with the noisy hinges and closes it behind her, so he can retreat to his studio with his memories of her body and move on to create on the canvas the bodies of the crows he is enamored with—the crow perched on a corpse, the crow spreading its majestic wings over the city, the crow piercing its prey with its beak, the crow tied with a golden rope, the crow keeping watch over an office, the crow that might become an angel or a demon, an eggplant or a jackal, garlic cloves or music notes, an ass

or an owl, a bald head or a bowl, or whatever the whiteness of the

canvas demands—while he waits for her to come back or for the

next woman to show up at his door.

"There is a definite gaze on the female . . . and this gaze is controlling. The female is marked and sectioned off, and violence follows, either by death, exile, or the use of the body to create a new city" (Pippin 1999). This is one of the qualities Pippin envisions for the apocalypse.

He comes back from the kitchen with tea for them and a Turkish coffee for himself, and he and the friend are absorbed in conversation, exchanging news about the people they know, and she hears but does not hear what they are saying and keeps herself busy looking around: at sketches and clips from magazines and newspapers already yellow with age, at images of him or his work or interviews or reviews, at spray paints and tubes and brushes and an antique fan and a straw hat and piles of books, and he and the friend ask her if she'd mind if they worked for a while, and she says, no, no, of course I don't mind, go ahead, and they leave the room and go into the studio and leave her in the sprawl of objects and words and art.

She puts her tea glass down and walks around and reads bits of the newspaper columns and looks at his sketches, postcards, and notes to himself, finds quotes that are brilliant or banal and random words jotted here and there that do not mean anything to her but perhaps mean something to him, and she hears the voices of the two in the studio talking about the stillness of the model and the movement of the artist, the exhaling of the model and the inhaling of the artist, the immortality of the creation and the ephemerality of the creator, about her body and his visions for the

sculpture of her body, and she walks around and over to the chest
at the corner closest to the kitchen, where she notices a pile of
more recent newspapers, and she gets closer and sees highlighted
headlines, and she gets closer and sees that they are about the
statues gone missing, and she begins browsing, careful not to make
a noise, and stashed among the pages she finds a few upside-down,
handwritten notes in his slanted handwriting, which she tries to
read while trying not to move anything, and on one note she picks
out the words "unearthed, bronze, square, ears, mold, mother,
child, dealer, trash, fresh (flesh?), interview, night, police officers,
detective, open space, displaced, lover, crane, weight, mother,"
and she notices a long numbered list on another, of which she can
make out only: "What quality . . . share? What time . . . ? . . . was
about to. . . . Reactions and . . . of the officials? The value of bronze
per kilogram . . ." She can still hear the two of them fervently
discussing muscles and shades and sparkles and the gentleness of
the material, so she peeks at the third page, and right before her
eyes there is a simplified, hand-drawn map of a city marked with
red dots all over, and the dots are connected by lines or dotted lines,
and the lines are surrounded by bubbles and words and signs, and
she thinks about taking the map with her or better yet taking a
picture of it with her phone, which is in her purse, but before going
back to the couch for her purse, she puts everything on the shelf
back in its place, and as she unzips her purse to get her phone before

walking back to the pile and taking pictures as fast as she can, she

hears their voices and footsteps coming out of the studio,

and she curses her luck and their timing.

When they reappear, she is sitting down, holding her tea in one

hand, and she looks at him, wondering whether she could, whether

she should, bring up the issue, ask questions, but she cannot read

him, and she glances at the pile of newspapers with notes hidden

in between, and she glances back at him, and still she cannot read

him, and even if he has felt the weight of her glances, he does not

heed them and keeps cleaning his hand with a handkerchief already

saturated with crimson, and the friend is redoing her hair and says,

we need to rush if we want to get to our next rendezvous on time,

and she gets up, and the friend finishes her tea standing up, and

she grabs her things and walks toward him and says, it was great

to finally meet you in person and see your studio, thank you for

the tea, hope to see you again soon, and she reaches out to shake

his hand, and looking at his face up close, she notices how tired his

eyes are, how burdened, and as he moves the handkerchief to his

left hand and she takes his right in hers, she pauses, wondering

whether she should ask, whether she should tell, whether she

should talk. The friend interrupts the pause to say they really need

to get going, but she really needs to ask, she really needs to know,

so she begins to say something, but before she can get past her

mumbling to the questions she needs to ask, he releases her hand,

and she feels her fingers dangling in midair, and her ring, with its turquoise stone, feels looser on her finger, and as he takes a few steps toward the kitchen, she hears him muttering something under his breath, which she doesn't really catch. The friend nudges her, and they walk to the door, leaving him to clean the crimson color from his hands.

"Crime is an art, and sometimes art is a crime" (Bolaño, in an interview on Chilean television, quoted in López-Calvo 2015).

Whether we interpret dreams like the Greeks or the Sufis, as
messages from the gods or the other world and thus prophetic
and guiding, or believe, like the Mohaves and the Australian
Aborigines, that "everything important was first dreamed in order
to be" (Notley 2014), or think, in the Freudian tradition, that "all
the material making up the content of a dream is in some way
derived from experience, that is to say, has been reproduced or
remembered in the dream" (Freud 2010) or that *a dream is the
fulfilment of a wish"* (Freud 2010), or consider them, following
Jung and Maeder, *"a spontaneous self-portrayal, in symbolic form,
of the actual situation in the unconscious"* (Jung 2010), we cannot
deny the relation of dreams to the realities of our waking lives, to
our pasts and our futures. We need to excavate them just as we
excavate archives and memories. We need to record them, speak
them, and analyze them as part of our (hi)stories. This is why
those dreamt during or in the years following the events become
indispensable to their trans(re)lation.

corpse (34)
families keep their silence

Corpse (4)

Age: 21
Gender: Female
Occupation: Student at Tehran University, BA in management, last semester
Date of Death: 30 Khordad 1388 / 20 June 2009
Place of Death: Tehran
Time of Death: Around 4 a.m.
Cause of Death: Hard blow to the head
Date of Burial: 1 Tir 1388 / 22 June 2009
Place of Burial: Behesht-e Zahra Cemetery, Tehran

She, like the other youth, is concerned, restless.
The father is worried. The news they listened to last night was troubling. He asks the mother to tell their daughter not to go to campus that day. He fears that she will join the protests.
She has an exam. It is her last exam.
She wears a green headscarf.
She leaves.
After the exam, she joins the protesters in the street. She adjusts her scarf. Covering her nose. Against tear gas. Covering her face. Against recognition. Leaving only her eyes visible. Watching.
Hours later, she comes back home.
The father watches her. Silent, but happy as always, she combs her hair and applies makeup in front of the mirror.
She goes to her room.
3:00 a.m. The brother notices that her light is still on.
3:30 a.m. The brother decides to check on her on his way to the kitchen for water, but then he sees her light go off, and he is relieved.

The next morning the mother calls the father at work and summons him home.

She is dead. A corpse is lying in her bed, rigid and cold.

In the medical examiner's office, a doctor tells them the cause of death was a hard blow to the head. The doctor does not write this down. The official document records it as death due to natural causes. The doctor thus gives the parents the gift of taking the corpse of their daughter for burial.

The father speaks of her thick black hair. Of her beautiful black eyes. She was tall. She was an athlete. She was hardworking. She danced beautifully. She danced whenever she saw her parents concerned. The father speaks of her love for the father. The father speaks of his love for her, his only daughter. The father did his studies in France. The family returned so they could raise their kids in their home country, among loved ones, despite concerns for their future.

The ceremony on the seventh night following her death is attended by many. Her friends from university.

Her friends tell the parents about the incident at the protest scene. Men ran after her. A man brought down a baton on her head. She fell down. She took her head in her hands and cried out in pain. Her friends wanted to take her to the hospital. Someone warned them that hospitals were not safe. She gathered herself. She assured them she was fine. She went back home.

Security forces pay the parents a visit. Security forces ask if the parents have any complaints or questions. They order the parents to keep quiet.

The parents do not take the matter to court.

A year later, a friend writes a letter to the committee the defeated camp set up to identify victims of protest violence, which already has her on their list. She speaks of her friend's case. Wants people to know about her.

The father speaks a few years later. Still broken. Crying.

The mother has aged. Her blue eyes don't laugh anymore. She wonders if her daughter would've been happier if they had lived elsewhere.

The family is devastated. Their world has come to an end.

The father speaks of his daughter's face in the tomb. As if she were a bride.

The father wonders about her right to life. The father asks why he should be alive.

The father misses her, wants her name and her memory to remain alive.

She is survived by her parents and two brothers.

I make her keep looking for the bronze bodies while these bodies of flesh and blood begin to become their own statues in the landscape of my soul.

They lost their lives on the same streets I was on, at the same time. Seeking their material now in the labyrinths of the virtual world, I have resurrected them in words only to confine them anew within other tombstones, this time on the page, between the covers of a book, not even in their own language.

Survivor's guilt.

The role of chance. In one's life. In another's death.

Why do they become important in death when in life they were just a few among millions, their lives and beliefs lost amid so many others? What do we hope to learn from them?

Do we want to exonerate ourselves? Of what? Because we are alive and they are dead? Because we are still here and they are gone?

Why do we feel guilty? Isn't this the history of all uprisings? Some dying, some surviving?

How do the parents of those whose names are never mentioned feel? Do they keep silent out of fear? Might some remain silent in order to keep their dead for themselves?

How do the parents who fear speaking feel? How do they bear the weight of the untold stories? How do they bear the dead loved ones inside them, who feel more alive than the living around them?

How do the parents whose children's stories are told and retold feel? Do we remember the same way that mothers and fathers and brothers and sisters and lovers remember their dead?

If what they do is remembrance, what should we call what we do?

An old friend calls. Asks her to join him at the restaurant if she feels like it. Tells her he is meeting a man she might be interested in. Doesn't say more about him. 10:00 p.m. She gets there at 10:10. The curtains behind the windows are different than what she remembers. So is the sign. She brakes and looks for a parking spot. A valet approaches her. There was no valet the previous time. The door is closed. She rings the bell. She gives the server who opens the door the friend's name. He told her to do so. The server nods, invites her in, closes the door once again, and asks her to follow him. The interior has changed too. The plants and the simple tables and chairs are gone. Instead, there's a spectacle of black and gold and silver, classic wallpaper, ultramodern tableware, prints of pop art on the walls alongside heavy pleated curtains, uniforms embroidered with traditional paisley, low house music playing. Within this hodgepodge sit men and women who stare at her as if she has been dropped there from another planet, muscular men in expensive sportswear or stout men in suits who smoke hookah while fingering prayer beads, women who are thin and tan and have had nose jobs or cheek implants or lip injections, who wear high heels and tight pants under their manteaus and silk scarves, who look in their brand-name purses for cell phones or mirrors or lipstick. Men and women who stare at her intently but briefly, dismissing her quietly as if deciding she is not chic enough or made-up enough or sexy enough or woman enough for their party.

Mind the steps, says the server, pointing to the raised platform of the more private section, where the friend is sitting with two other men, one young and tall and fit, wearing casual clothes and lots of hair gel, the other middle-aged and tall and fit, wearing a suit and almost bald. On their table are tea and sweets, and a hookah sits on the floor next to each man. He sees her and stands up, and the other two follow, but only halfway. She sits down, and he orders another hookah just for her, the tobacco a special cocktail mix they import just for the restaurant, he says, and he introduces the younger man as the head chef and doesn't introduce the older one, and the head chef simply smiles at her and tells him something about not forgetting to buy him the gold watch, the latest model, the one with the black hands, with the chronometer, before it's out of stock, and he excuses himself, but not before telling her that she should try the special, the saffron rice and lamb stew, and if not, definitely the filet mignon with pomegranate sauce, and the friend orders iceberg-lettuce salad, which he knows she likes, and one of each of those dishes, and he asks the chef to choose one other and says they are going to share them all, and as the chef leaves, the friend introduces the other man, not by his name but by his job title, bank manager, and he then mentions that he's in charge of the purchase of artwork for the bank's private collection, and she understands why she is here tonight.

"[Pumla] Gobodo-Madikizela [who served on the South African Truth and Reconciliation Commission] suggests that collecting stories not only of harm but also of context, and of the drawn-out effects of violence and unjust systems, may in some settings shed more light on what the problems are and how they might be addressed and redressed than would a legal trial" (Stauffer 2015).

corpse (40)
identities forged

How important is this gesture of exposing and narrating?
Does it really reshape the power structures? Is it really dangerous
to the status quo?
Are those who expose heroes, or are they traitors?
What is in the naming of those who expose: whistleblowers, spies,
researchers, journalists, confessors, shamans, seers, witches, leaders,
storytellers?
What are their stories?
How can we trust? The witness, the exposer, the words, the
documents, the evidence, the freedom?
How can we trust when we can't even trust the self and its
memories?

corpse (41)
martyrs confiscated

The Iranian regime, which during the years of the Iran–Iraq War flourished by exploiting the culture of martyrdom, now refuses the dead of the Green Movement the same title. They are not to be called martyrs, officially or unofficially, by friends and family, or even on their tombstones.

What to do in the face of a regime that exploits and manipulates not just narratives of life but also narratives of death?

What to do when the dead of a movement become martyrs for various causes, used by different parties, governments, regimes, each to its own end?

What to do with a society that thrives on the culture of martyrdom? The word "martyr" comes from the Greek root "mártus," meaning "witness." Similarly, in Persian, both "testimony" and "martyrdom" are expressed with one word: شهادت ("shahaadat"). The word for "witness" is شاهد ("shaahed"), and the word for "martyr" is شهید ("shaheed"). Both words come from the same Arabic root and are variations of the three letters ش ه د : "shaahed" ("witness") is in the Arabic subject form, meaning someone who does something, and "shaheed" ("martyr") is in the Arabic exaggerated noun form, meaning someone who does something or possesses a quality to a great degree. Martyr as a mighty witness, even on a linguistic level.

Perhaps the regime refuses to name the dead as martyrs because they don't want the lost women and men of the opposition associated with religious causes. Or perhaps it's because they don't want them to bear witness and testify, even on a linguistic level, to the atrocities inflicted upon them. The regime that has already erased them from the physicality of the present moment now wants to erase them from history as well.

The fate and responsibility of the dead/martyrs as witnesses are tightly woven to that of other witnesses, writers or poets, who give "strength of proof to what in itself lacks it and [grants] life to what could not live alone" (Agamben 2002). Testimony is "always an act of an 'author'" and "the poetic word is the one that is always situated in the position of a remnant and that can, therefore, bear witness" (Agamben 2002). It is for these very reasons that, especially in sites of horror and erasure, the role of journalists, artists, and writers becomes of utmost significance, and for these very reasons that they are censored, threatened, and silenced, figuratively or literally.

The man doesn't look at her but rather fumbles with his cell phone for a while, and she and the friend begin catching up and smoking their hookahs and sipping their green juices and picking at the salad before he finally looks at her, and when he does, she sees in his eyes a curiosity, a cupidity, a softness that's not without violence, and a smile forms at their corners, and she puffs at her hookah and asks him about the bank's latest acquisition, asks whose work they have purchased so far, asks what kind of work they are interested in, and he puffs at his hookah and tells her he can't say, tells her he might later, tells her instead about the building that is being renovated to house the collection, about the ancient Quran that they've just received as a gift and that will be the centerpiece of the opening, though of course he can't name the donor, explains that their mission is to support artists and the national art scene, and gives her numbers and prices and statistics without taking his eyes off her, as if he wants to observe the effect of his words. The saffron rice and the lamb stew and the filet mignon with the pomegranate sauce and a vegetarian pasta dish arrive, and the waiter arranges the food on the table, and the chef comes back to say bon appétit, and she busies herself with the food, and the friend shows the man something on his phone, and she wonders what she can say to find out if he has any leads, and another waiter arrives

with fresh coal for the hookahs, and the two men busy themselves

with the food and with talk about last night's UEFA Champions

League soccer match, and she busies herself with her food and her

cell phone, and the three of them exchange pleasantries from time

to time, and the two men keep patting each other's backs, and she

smokes her hookah and drinks her black tea and looks at the man,

who has been watching her as if he's appraising another artwork

he might buy, and she decides to simply ask him about the statues,

but right then his phone blips, and he looks at it, and his face

changes as he looks, and he gets closer to the friend and mumbles

something in his ear, and the two of them laugh the laughter of

men who think the world revolves around their masculinity, and

she takes a long, deep puff at her hookah, and he gets up and grabs

his prayer beads and his second cell phone and his wallet and looks

at her, saying he hopes to see her soon, that maybe next time he

can host her at his place, and she moves the coals on her hookah

around and puffs out the smoke stuck inside and does no more

than nod, and as he takes his leave the friend orders another

round of tea for the two of them.

"The processes of expressing and making public the interpretations and meanings of those [traumatic] pasts are extremely dynamic, as these interpretations and meanings are never fixed once and for all. They change over time, following a complex logic that combines the temporality of the expression and of the working through and acting out of trauma . . . , the explicit political strategies of various actors, and the questions, answers, and conversations introduced in the public sphere" (Jelin 2003).

Corpse (5)

Age: 43
Gender: Male
Date of Death: 6 Dey 1388 / 27 December 2009
Place of Death: Tehran
Time of Death: Around 3:00 p.m.
Cause of Death: Assassination
Date of Burial: 9 Dey 1388 / 30 December 2009
Place of Burial: Behesht-e Zahra Cemetery, Tehran

Large crowds in the streets. The Day of Ashura. Mourners and protesters mingle. The sounds of religious chants and political slogans mingle.

Smiling, he tells his wife not to worry, that he'll be back soon.

He is the nephew of the presidential candidate who later becomes the leader of the Green Movement. He is not a politician. He supports his uncle's presidential campaign and later takes part in the protests surrounding the election results.

Nephew and uncle have a close relationship.

He fought in Kurdistan, in the Shalamcheh area, during the Iran–Iraq war. He was only fifteen or sixteen years old at the time.

He walks to the main street close by to see how things are going. A black Nissan Patrol drives by fast. The sound of gunshots. The car hits people. The driver and passengers in the Nissan Patrol all wear black.

A reporter later describes the driver: a man who appeared to be between thirty and thirty-five, fair-skinned, reddish hair, thick reddish beard. The two passengers wore beards as well.

Another witness later describes him as a man of twenty, fair-skinned.

Someone running tells the wife, who's waiting worried at the door, that someone has been shot. She knows it. She feels it. She immediately tells her daughter that her husband, their father, has been shot.

Someone later reports the bullet was fired from a Colt at very close range.

The police attack people in the alley. The wife and daughter run inside the house.

He comes back. Carried by people. Shot.

In the street, the car follows people around.

Pedestrians flee to the sidewalks.

Sounds of more bullets being fired.

The car runs people over. The car flees the scene.

The hallway of the house.

His voice. He says he is thirsty.

Voices of men and women. Uncertain. Unsure. Chaos.

Someone is filming the scene. A woman begs the person filming not to film. The man swears he won't film faces.

Lying on the white tile floor by the staircase.

The film on YouTube shows only his legs and the legs of the people surrounding him, shows his body only up to his neck.

People around him trying to figure out what to do.

Someone asks about the position of the bullet.

He breathes heavily.

Honey. Someone asks him to stick out his tongue, wants to put some honey on his tongue.

Women and men talking, asking questions, wondering, desperate.

Black pants and shirt. Black coat. White undershirt soaked in blood.

A bullet in his chest, close to his neck.

Heavy breathing. Moaning.

Someone mentions the presence of a nurse, a head nurse.

People around him trying to find a way to care for him.

Someone asks for the lights to be turned on.

Heavy breathing. Moaning.

Careful not to touch the area of the wound.

Someone mentions finding a car, taking him to the emergency room. A woman fears his arrest in the hospital.

Keeping people at a distance, giving him space.

People trying to move his legs, his body, his head to a better position.

Someone calls for a pillow.

Voices of protesters outside.

Someone asks for the door to the house to be shut.

Heavy breathing. Moaning.

Someone asks that something be put under his feet.

The Day of Ashura. No one expected bullets to be fired. Anger.

Someone mentions his relationship to the leader. A pillow.

He asks them to put something under his head, to lift it a bit higher.

A car waiting at the door.

Protesters close by.

A woman pleads with them not to take him to the hospital. Cries. Terrified. Says she won't let them take him away.

His bare back. His white undershirt. White floor tiles.

She mentions his relationship to the leader.

Someone hushes her, says not to mention names on camera.

She says she won't allow them to take him away. She fears his arrest.

A man snaps at her. He is bleeding. He needs to be taken to the hospital.

Voices of men. One telling the other to shut up. That he is bleeding.

His voice.

He says he is suffocating.

Heavy breathing. Moaning.

He says he is suffocating.

A private hospital. Not a public one.

She lets out a wail.

No faces. Only voices. And legs.

A car at the door. People crowd around. They put him in the car.

Streets are busy. People are protesting. Traffic is heavy. It takes awhile to get him to the hospital.

A burning sensation in his back. Thirst.

He recites the prayer of death.

He dies before reaching the hospital, his head on the lap of his brother-in-law, who rides with him in the car. According to other reports, he dies at the hospital.

People are already gathering at the hospital. Shouting their condolences to the leader.

Police and militia are already at the hospital.

A few hours at the hospital.

His dead body lies in the hospital morgue.

People disperse. To go pay their respects to his mother and uncle. People gather.

At the house everyone is wearing black. At the house everyone is crying. The leader. The mother.

The leader is asked to make a statement regarding the death. He refuses, noting that his nephew is just one among many killed and should not be treated differently.

The body disappears from the hospital.

The police deny the disappearance. They say the body is at the medical examiner's office for further investigation because of the suspicious circumstances surrounding the death.

The phone rings three days after the shooting. An unknown voice says they can come pick up the body for burial.

He is buried under strict security measures. Only family members are allowed to be present.

He was a kind, calm, loving man. He was trusted and loved by many; many confided in him. He did what he could for others.

His family receives visits and condolences from people, politicians, clergymen.

He was threatened a few times in the days preceding the shooting.

The police announce that he was the target of an organized terrorist attack. They announce that the revolver and the bullets used were professional-grade materials of anti-revolution terrorist groups. They identify the owner of the car. The owner announces that the car was stolen from him a few days before the incident. They arrest him for further investigation, as up until then he had not reported the theft.

Some claim the shooting was arranged by the leader's own camp as a tactic to give their unjust movement momentum.

The case remains unresolved.

He is survived by his mother, his sister, his wife, a daughter (seventeen at the time of his death), and a son (seven at the time of his death).

What is the role of oral history in this translating, archiving, retelling?
What is the role of the visual history found in pictures and videos
online?
What about written documents?
What would we have today to refer to, to cling to, without
journalists, without citizen journalists, exiled or imprisoned or
living life just as before?
Whose words should be considered trustworthy? How can truths
be separated from lies?
Are the truths perceived at the moment of death one and the
same as the truths perceived at the moment of burial, on the first
anniversary, in the years after?
Are the truths for the generation that has lived the experience
the same as the truths for the generation preceding it? For the
generation inheriting it?
How do we access the truths of different times? The times that
belong to us? Those that don't?
What does it mean for a time to belong to us? For us to belong to
a time?
How do we pass on the truths of each?
How do we fight the myth of the one and only Truth?
How to move from the Truth to truths?
Who defines truths? Our truths?
Embodying these truths, who do we become?
Embodying these truths, who do the dead become?
How can we know what the dead would have wanted? What if they
don't want to be engraved in the minds of people? What if they
don't want to be heroes? Do we allow them the right to choose?
What would that even look like? Do we stop and wonder for a
moment who we are to decide for them, for their narratives?
Do we seek refuge in the certainty of dead bodies to defend
ourselves against the uncertainties of the future?

Corpse (6)

Age: 36
Gender: Male
Occupation: Laborer and blogger
Education: Secondary school degree
Date of Arrest: 9 Aban 1391 / 30 October 2012
Date of Death: 13 Aban 1391 / 3 November 2012
Place of Death: Cyber Police detention center, Tehran
Time of Death: Unknown
Cause of Death: Controversial
Date of Burial: 17 Aban 1391 / 7 November 2012
Place of Burial: Imamzadeh Mohammad Taghi Cemetery, Robat Karim

He is arrested by the Cyber Police. Around noon. His house in Robat Karim, where he lives with his mother. His hands tied behind him.
The mother and father are separated. He is the breadwinner of the house; he takes care of his mother.
When the mother asks if they have a warrant, one officer shows her his gun.
He is taken away, along with his laptop and papers. When the mother asks, she is told he is being taken to Tehran. No further information is given.
Some days before the arrest, he spoke to a friend about visits from the police, who searched the house and confiscated his notebooks, of hoping to leave the country if problems arise, of not having yet been subpoenaed, of not fearing an arrest, of being concerned only about his mother's well-being. He said, "If they come for me right now telling me they are to put the rope around my neck, I say this death is more honorable than this life, this life in

shame. Because this is not life we are living, this is slavery."

On his blog he writes about the suffering of the people, of economic and social problems, of unemployment and prostitution. He writes in support of the imprisoned female lawyers and activists. He writes about human rights. He writes against state oppression.

In one of his last posts, he writes of the threats: that his mother will soon have to wear black, since he won't stop talking, that he needs to shut up or else be shut up, that not even his name will remain, that no one will know what has befallen him.

The Cyber Police consider his blog propaganda against the state, insulting its values and virtues, spreading false news, cooperating with enemy activists outside the country.

After his arrest, he is sent to Evin Prison, from which he is quickly transferred to a Cyber Police detention center. There, four days after his arrest, he dies.

A week after the arrest, the son-in-law receives a phone call.

The son-in-law goes where he is told.

He is asked if the prisoner had any illnesses. He says no, none. He is informed that the prisoner is dead. He asks why. He is slapped across the mouth, shouted at to shut up, to not ask questions, told that they are the ones who ask questions.

He is told to inform the sister and the mother. He is told to go buy a cemetery plot, to arrange the transfer of the body and the burial for the following morning.

The family is told that he died of a heart attack.

Forty-one prisoners write a statement. Testifying to signs of torture on his body, to his fear of being killed when transferred.

Another statement made by himself. Written while he was in Evin, on an official prison form, two days prior to his death. A complaint to the prison officials. Testifying to being tortured and holding the Cyber Police responsible in case something happens to him.

The attorney general raises several doubts about his statement, about its authenticity and content, about its circulation outside the prison.

The mother and sister speak out.

The sister is proud of the late brother. The sister swears to his innocence. Asks why. Says he will be forever alive. Demands not to be sent condolences. Demands to be congratulated. The sister cries.

The mother says she has lost her son on the path of God. Says she's not sorrowful. Speaks of his health, of his never having taken any painkillers. Says that not once could she speak to him following his arrest.

When the media covers the news, the family's phone lines get blocked. The family is told to remain silent. A reporter in exile calls to talk. To Cyber Police officials. The person on the phone denies the case, says he has not heard of it, says she'll have to come in person to inquire about any case.

On the third day after the burial, the mother is called in to meet her son's killers. A man sits before her and tells her.

The son laughed in the face of their threats during interrogations. The son was tied to the chair and tortured more and more intensely the harder he laughed.

The interrogator asks for forgiveness.

The mother is shown an official warrant and told that if she does not sign a form indicating that she has no complaints against the officials, her daughter will be arrested. The same warrant is shown to the brother and the son-in-law, who are waiting outside.

According to some, the head of the body in the shroud had a big dent in it and was covered here and there with plaster. The face of the body was bloated. The knee of the body was bloody. There were signs of an autopsy. There was blood all over the shroud.

A month after the death, the father is admitted to the hospital, seemingly as a result of an emotional breakdown.

On the fortieth day after the burial, a ceremony at his grave. A picture of him. A bowl of dates. A bowl of apples and oranges and bananas. Flower petals cover the gravestone. Wreaths stand to one side.

A man cries at the grave, wondering out loud, "Why are there no condolence banners from neighbors? For the death of the man always thinking of others in need?" Wondering out loud, "How will his sister endure this?"

A woman wails.

The mother and sister hold up pictures of him and walk around the cemetery. They are proud of the man they have lost. They call out the names of other young men and women killed, the names of their mothers. The sister says he lost his life for Iran, says that's a worthwhile death. The sister recites poetry, says she will not cry, for he is a hero. The mother cries.

Mothers of other lost children surround them.

A mother tells. Of a son lost fourteen years ago. Of a body never recovered.

Both mothers ask, "Why?" Each mother calls the name of the other's son.

All the mothers cry.

As the family gets ready to leave the cemetery, the police raid begins. The brother is taken out of the car and arrested for filming with his cell phone. The mother and the sister are beaten. The brother is let go a few hours later, after his phone has been confiscated. (This brother is referenced only in one other instance.)

A member of the parliament speaks out against torture in prisons and the silence that follows. He believes these things are harmful to the image of the regime, that they disgrace the blood of the martyrs of war. He demands an official investigation.

The judiciary branch announces the beginning of an official investigation.

The father hires a lawyer. The family files a lawsuit. Reports on the tortures and cause of death provided by different officials throughout the investigation are inconsistent:

No signs of torture or bruises, death due to natural causes. Prisoners can die of natural causes.

Five bruises on the body, on the left shoulder and leg, on the right knee and wrist, but no sign of anything unnatural with regard to the head, neck, and internal organs, including the heart, lungs, and genitals.

Sudden and natural death, probably as a result of a heart failure caused by stress or psychological problems.

Official report to the parliament: the arrest was carried out with an official judicial warrant.

The medical examiner's office releases its final decision on the cause of death: the exact cause of death is unknown. None of the blows to the body were lethal or aimed at the body's sensitive areas. No signs of poisoning. No signs of illness. No signs of any external causes. The office thus considers the most probable cause of death to be shock due to a combination of psychological pressure and physical blows.

A few officers, including the man the mother has met, are arrested.

The head of the Tehran Cyber Police is removed from his position.

Later on, the mother speaks about the son's fingers, which appeared broken during the corpse washing. The mother believes the crooked handwriting in the statement he wrote in the prison confirms that the fingers were broken. No official reports mention broken fingers.

Later on, one report announces that the cause of death was physical shock, that his testicles were burnt and injured.

Later on, a medical examiner's report, which has all along been among the documents in the case file to which the lawyer has just received access, reveals he had internal bleeding in the lungs, the liver, the kidneys, and the cerebellum. Independent doctors consider this and the resulting lack of oxygen the cause of death.

The mother demands the body be exhumed.

The mother continues to speak.

The mother calls him her "everything." He took care of the mother, buying all her medicine on the black market, laboring to provide for her. He was generous and helped other laborers in need.

The mother visits the cemetery, gets lifts from the townspeople. She spends the days at his grave and the nights with his photographs. The mother is visited by other mothers who have lost. On the mantelpiece in her living room, she keeps pictures of several of the imprisoned and the killed. The mother cries for all and asks for justice for all.

The mother becomes a symbol of resistance. A voice for the lost children. For the surviving mothers.

The sister continues to speak.

The sister is threatened in the street. A motorcyclist tells her to stop talking or she'll end up where her brother ended up.

The father disappears. For ten days, no one knows of his whereabouts. Upon his return, police physicians diagnose him with Alzheimer's. The lawyer considers the diagnosis suspicious and demands an examination by independent doctors. She is wary that the diagnosis might impede the course of the legal case, for which the father is the official plaintiff.

A year later, the interrogator is indicted for second-degree murder, sentenced to imprisonment and lashes. The family and the lawyer oppose the court procedure and ruling. They relinquish the case. They reject the blood money.

The father dies three years later. At his burial, the sister speaks. Of the brother and the father. Of the father's heart attack three days after the brother's death. Of the father now resting in peace with the brother. The sister recites poetry. The mother speaks.

He is survived by his mother, his sister (married with a baby son at the time of his death), and a brother (or two, according to some sources).

Who was the last to see the body? Who washed the corpse? Does the corpse washer remember washing the body? Does the corpse washer remember the corpses of protesters differently than the other corpses?

How do families continue to live the love, the loss, the memories, the wounds, the pains?

Are the accounts of the close survivors objective?

Is objectivity even the point?

Isn't subjectivity at the root of all history, at the root of all storytelling?

Whose subjectivity?

Shouldn't we aim for inclusion of all subjectivities instead of one objectivity?

How do we fight against the dangers of fixed frames, fixed narratives?

How can we open ourselves to the pain of embracing all narratives?

The further we go on together, the more I desire to expose her to these other bodies, divert her from the living ones she's surrounded herself with, the bronze ones she's searching for. I want to sit her down and tell her she needs to search for these bodies instead, needs to get to know them, their (hi)stories, intimately, needs to ask questions.

I know there is value in the living bodies. I know there is value in bodies of art, and in the search for them, too. And I know she must already know about the other bodies, the dead bodies: they've lived through the same times, the same events, within the same borders; they've also shared space between the covers of this book, even if their paths have not yet crossed.

I know all that, but I also know one can know of something without truly knowing it, a knowing that results from reaching out, searching, documenting, getting intimate with, embodying. For that, I think I'll wait a bit longer, wait until I'm certain she's ready. But then I wonder: Will I ever be certain about such a decision? Will she ever be ready for such truths?

Part of me wants to protect her, save her from the pain that you and I have come to face. Part of me wants to spare her from the brutality of reality, like a mother who doesn't know any better. Perhaps I should just let her find her way to the stories, or let the stories find their way to her. In their own way, in their own time.

corpse (43)
escape

What happens to the other narratives, the ones that escape us while we're busy digging into these narratives and these voices? Are they lost forever?

What to do as the voices from the past recede further and further into the past?

Is this the very thing that allows us to go on living? Or is it the very reason we are doomed?

The sun is getting ready to set behind the high-rises and the mountains as she and the lover set off for a friend's ski lodge to spend a few hours away from the city. The sun sets, the roads meander, the mountains rise, the sky spreads, the valleys fall, and the snow unfurls across the mountains, the roads, the valleys, its blue and white and gray and brown crawling into one another before their thirst for the land and the air separates them, before the force of cement and glass and plastic and metal and brick and gravel and asphalt separates them, before they find their way back into an embrace once again. The roads take them away, away from the mutilated air of a city lying on its deathbed, suffocating its people with the dark, heavy blanket of smog, a blanket they themselves keep threading with an avarice for apartments and malls and buildings and cars and highways and apartments and malls and buildings and cars, suffocating them as they walk and drive and rush and live and die and live and die and die and die. The roads take them away: into the naked air that shall not remain naked much longer, that shall soon be covered, because the blanket is growing larger and heavier, the boundaries between the city and the country disappearing, nature disappearing, the human's legs spreading wider and wider, his voice rising louder and louder. The roads take them away so their bodies can spend a few hours in the arms of the solemn snow, so their cheeks can be blushed by the oxygen and the food and the company and the freshness and the coldness of the air. Only to send them back to the city a few hours later.

The stars shine, and the dogs bark, and the snow sparkles, and they move toward the darkness and heaviness of the blanket. She sits in the passenger seat clutching the unknown pain in her stomach, and he heads straight to a twenty-four-hour clinic, and she sits in the colorful chairs of the waiting room, feeling uncomfortable and restless, and he pays the admission fees, and they wait only a minute or so before the doctor calls her in, as soon as two other patients have left the room, and she tells him about the pain and that she had thought it was her period but now she doesn't think so anymore, that she had thought it had gotten better after she took a pill late last night, that she woke up fine this morning and was fine not eating anything during the day, was fine until after taking that one bite for dinner, and now she thinks she should not have taken even that one bite, thinks it might have been something she ate at the restaurant last night, thinks she should perhaps not have smoked the hookah last night, and oh, the pain is really awful, and the tears fall down her face, and she clutches her purse and the chair and almost shouts.

156

The doctor examines her, says he can't tell what's causing the spasms and the pain, says he'll prescribe a few things and that the nurse will inject her in the next room. He suggests she lie down for an IV because she hasn't eaten, and her blood pressure is low, and it won't take longer than half an hour, and meanwhile the shots will take care of the spasms and the pain, and after that they'll see how she's doing. She thanks the doctor. She shuts the door. The nurse reopens the door to usher someone else in. White tiles cover the hallway's floor. The nurse looks into a half-open cabinet of drugs and picks out some medication. The nurse shows her to the next room. Curtains separate the beds. She lies down on a bed next to the wall. She bends in pain. The nurse gives her the shots. The nurse looks for a vein in her arm. She curls in pain. She screams. The nurse fails. The nurse looks for a vein in her hand. The nurse finds the vein and puts in the IV. She sobs. He comes in to caress her, to soothe her, to whisper to her, to hold her hand. The IV drips into her. The pain subsides a bit, but not really. He goes out. She listens to the sounds of the men and women coming and going outside in the hallway and listens to the nurse and the doctor talking, then the nurse comes in while on the phone with someone else, who seems to be a woman, and checks up on her, and the iv drips some more, and the nurse goes to the other side of the curtain and tells the friend on the phone that she's having guests tomorrow and that the maid cannot make it and asks if the friend can come over to help with food preparation, and the iv drips some more, and the nurse leaves the room, leaves her with the beds and the curtains and the walls, and nobody comes in for a while. Only a few more drops of the medication are left in the iv's plastic container, and the half hour is gone, and the pain is not.

He comes in and caresses her face, her hair, her arm, her hand, her neck, her cheeks and talks of this and that, and she cries and curses, and he goes out to ask for the doctor again. The nurse comes in. The nurse takes the iv needle out, injects two more drugs. The doctor comes in. The doctor tells her to go home and rest a bit, assuring her the shots will take care of her, tells her to go to the hospital if the pain gets worse during the night. The doctor leaves. He comes in to help her get ready to leave.

She feels the urge to throw up. She feels the pain squeezing everything inside her, squeezing hard even when it subsides. He asks if she needs something to throw up in, if he should call the nurse or the doctor. She says no, no, telling herself it will go away, it will go away. He begins to gather her things. She feels the pain stabbing into her, deep into her. He waits for her at the door. She wants to reach inside herself, grab her guts, and get rid of it all, wants to throw up and empty herself of the weight of the pain. She runs to the sink at the corner of the room, and she retches, thinking who is going to clean up this mess, this mess, this vomit.

160

She decides she needs a massage. A full body massage. Maybe a facial. Maybe a manicure and a pedicure. Maybe a haircut, but not a new color. It's just one of those days. She calls the spa and, miraculously, is able to get in for a manicure and a haircut. No appointments available for a massage and a facial for a month, the receptionist tells her. Not enough time for both a pedicure and a manicure with the woman she has asked for. She pays the old man who has made it his job to help the women park on the street and watch their cars while they're inside having their bodies attended to, and as she buzzes and enters the building, beyond the brownish-gray curtain separating the women-only inside from the outside, she is welcomed by the sound of water flowing down a wall into a small pool and the scent of incense in the air. Today, for a few hours, she will spoil herself the way many of the women here do several times a week, stealing away from the company or the hospital or the school or the office or the home to attend to their bodies on the occasion of a dinner party, a birthday party for one of their kids' playmates, a wedding, an engagement party, a vacation to one foreign beach or another, a gallery opening, a rendezvous with a lover, or simply because they feel down or are bored with one hair color or nail polish or have too many free hours on hand.

The haircut doesn't take that long. The stylist knows her hair, her style, her likes and dislikes. A few snips here and there. A touch of the razor here and there. The same cut invigorated. As she hugs her and thanks her for her magic touch, the stylist tells her that in two months, she'll be heading back to L.A. for good, or at least for the time being, in case she wants to make another appointment before then. She says of course she will and asks her if she's on Facebook so that they can befriend one another later but they still exchange email addresses just in case.

Downstairs, in the nail salon, she lets the fingers of one hand linger in the water bowl while those of the other rest in the hand of her favorite manicurist in town, who knows exactly how she likes her nails filed, not too square, not too round. The young woman tells her that she and her husband have decided to live a bit longer at her in-laws' to save up for their apartment, tells her about his new business, tells her she loves her new haircut, asking which of the stylists upstairs did it for her, asking why she never lets it grow long, asking why she never tries highlights or lowlights, the difference between which the manicurist has to explain to her, tells her about a new oil she's tried for stronger nails, suggests she try it too, asks what she has been up to since they last met, tells her she might be able to change her toenail polish, too, if her next customer shows up late.

Women's feet idle and age in the hot water in custom-designed sinks, and their hands and fingers are massaged, and their nails are painted black or French or beige or dark blue or purple or different shades of red, cherry or toxic red or blood orange or divine passion or simply red, or each finger is painted a different color of the rainbow. A pack of digestive biscuits is offered by another manicurist who has lost many kilos since she was last here and is passed around the room from one free hand to another, and she explains to the curious eyes who her doctor is, how hard the diet is, how long the hours at the gym are, how she has had to go shopping for new clothes, smaller sizes, different styles.

The receptionist calls her manicurist to let her know the next customer has canceled, and the manicurist fills the sink with fresh hot water for her feet, adding a few drops of Betadine, and she takes off her shoes and socks and happily dips her feet into the hot water. She can now continue to eavesdrop on the not-so-quiet conversations the other women are having. One speaks of the latest ISIS attacks, taking her analysis back to 9/11, then all the way to the UN's and Russia's latest moves with regard to Syria, moving from Afghanistan to Turkey to Saudi Arabia to Britain to the U.S., talking as if she's a political analyst expert in the region's dilemmas and aims to solve them once and for all before her nail polish dries. The timid elderly server walks in with her tray and circles the room asking if anyone would like tea or coffee, and the receptionist calls to let one of the girls know her lunch order has been delivered, and the girl excuses herself for a second and comes back with a plastic bag, the contents smelling of burgers and fries, and she hands it to the server and asks her to put it, please, in the kitchen for now, and her manicurist takes a moment to check the text messages on her phone, the smile on her face suggesting she's sending a heart or a smiley or their text equivalents to her husband, then cuffs her pant legs and pushes them up and begins massaging her feet with lavender and almond oil, and as she closes her eyes, letting her muscles relax under the manicurist's strong fingers, she hears the two women sitting in front of her speak, like several others in the room, about their kids.

One woman wonders if she should order cupcakes and balloons for her youngest child's birthday party or go with the caterer they used for their eldest child's party, who handles everything from decorations to finger foods to dinner to the cake to party favors for kids and parents, and the two go on and on discussing which choices would make the party the talk of the town, and right when she's on the verge of asking her manicurist to hurry up so she can get out of there before they drive her insane with their pretentious luxuries, one of them, not the one throwing the party, says something about how amazing it would be if she could arrange a tour of the doll museum she took her daughter and a few of her friends to a month ago, which they loved and talked about the entire week after with their friends at school, and the woman who wants to throw a party gets excited and says, oh, that's an amazing idea, I can have the kids' nanny and tutor take them there and then have the party later at home, but the other rushes to add, yes, it would be amazing, but unfortunately she doesn't think it is possible anymore, since the other day while she was waiting at the bank, she heard on national news that the museum was broken into the night before, and along with the office equipment and cameras, more than a hundred dolls were stolen, so she doesn't think it's worth the visit anymore even if the museum is open, and the other woman gets disappointed and wonders once again what to do for the party, how to make sure it is à la mode enough for the pictures she wants the photographer she's hiring to take of her beautiful family and of the event, and the two begin once again to evaluate the work of one event planner against another, to compare the party one mother threw to that of another and another, while the one who delivered the news of the dolls being stolen doesn't cease to remind the other how memorable the visit she arranged to the museum was for the daughter and her friends, oh well, I guess nobody else can experience that now, I'm glad I did that for them, oh, they still get so excited when they tell their friends about it at school, oh, I wish you could do it, too, but I guess you can't anymore.

In the Nazi camps, the tortured bodies could not be named as such. "Under no circumstances were they to be called 'corpses' or 'cadavers,' but rather simply Figuren, figures, dolls" (Agamben 2002).

She thinks about asking the woman if she knows anything else about the dolls, but then she decides she has better chances of finding information on the internet, since the woman wouldn't have heard any news of it if she hadn't happened to be waiting at the bank, if the TV hadn't been set on the national news channel, if it wasn't time for the local news.

Her manicurist finishes up her foot massage and cleans the oil from her nails with alcohol and asks what color she wants today, and thinking about the gray dress and the colorful, flowery heels she wants to wear to the party tonight, she asks for the reddest red they have, for both her hands and her feet.

It's all subjective, relative. Whom we judge and why and how. She judges the women throwing parties for their kids, their self-absorbed grandiosity. I judge her half-serious search, her caring but not caring enough. Someone else judges me, and I judge myself, and the chain continues.

Who am I to be translating, rebuilding, representing, recounting, relating these people, these events, these narratives, these truths, these worlds?

Do I have permission to speak these stories?

Are they my stories? Are they my stories too?

"I do not know how to talk about my country without talking about all the bodies it has destroyed. I do not know how to talk about my city without talking about all the bodies it keeps underground. I do not know how to talk about ghosts without talking about myself" (Borzutzky 2015).

What purpose can these narratives fulfill when at some point they'll become another object of intellectual inquiry on a library shelf, another object that's lost its emotional bearings? What good is yet another remnant? Of a time, of a people, of a hope for change, or a struggle against hopelessness?

How do disparate attempts at storytelling become our collective narratives, our collective memories?

How can a narrative be collective when each of us reads and remembers it through our individual bodies and minds and emotions? Through our individual (hi)stories? How can a narrative be collective when we are constantly shedding cells and new ones are appearing in their place?

What to do to move beyond judgment, beyond criticism? To move beyond separations and toward shared spaces?

How do collective narratives become collective actions? How much time does it take?

Is a compilation of stories that leads to noise better or worse than silence?
Doesn't noise create the illusion of knowledge, sympathy, empathy?
Of narratives heard, existences registered, lessons learned?
Why this need for words?
Why not silence?
Is silence ignorance? Is silence rejection? Is silence stagnation?
Doesn't silence hint at the void? At the sacred? At the unspeakable?
Can't silence be sacred?

corpse (44)
men in armor

She is excited for the friend's party tonight. The lover is late to pick her up. He is supposed to buy dessert. She has already gotten the friend two tiny bowls, azure inside and white outside, filled with the tiny traditional flowers she knows she loves. This is her housewarming and a celebration of her thesis defense. This is her own place after a hard divorce. This is the result of her years-long research on the subject of marriage satisfaction and psychology. This is her friend getting back on her feet, and she's happy to be sharing in the celebration.

She knows the neighborhood. Only a short drive away. Once upon a time, a village adjacent to a past city. Now just another neighborhood interweaving with others to form a transient map of the present city. Of its deeply rooted trees, only some remain. Of its large gardens, many are gone. The fabric store, the hardware store, the hookah store, the copy shop, the car stereo store, the handwoven rug store, the confectionery, the sandwich shop are all still there, exactly as they were once upon a time, or as ghosts of their older selves, reinvented for new customers and their demands. The little old groceries are now little supermarkets. The flower shop has new tiles and paint, and its window is filled with orchids and houseplants. The bakery still bakes its barbari bread but in an electric stove instead of a coal one. The bread doesn't taste the same. The butcher shop is still there, though the carcasses of the cows and calves and sheep and lambs and chickens don't dangle from hooks in front of the store anymore, but are skinned and deboned and cleaned and sliced and portioned and marinated in the basement, which has been renovated according to the health authorities' rules and regulations, and only then is the meat brought up to be arranged in constantly sanitized containers and fridges and showcases. The mosque is still there, too, trying to hold on to its past splendor. And so are the mountains and the mountain paths and the mountaineers and the river flowing through the mountains and their valleys, the cafés and the sunny-side-ups and the lentil soups served with hot bread and freshly brewed tea. Though perhaps even the mountains and their paths and the river and the mountaineers and the cafés are not the same anymore. They pass a few body shops and the neighborhood's taftoon bakery, whose bread she loves and buys whenever she passes, if there's not a long line, and then they reach the friend's building, right in front of the sports complex, and find a parking spot near some construction waste piled up in a corner, and as she notices the shadows of the prison gate further up the road she wraps her long, black satin veil around her bare legs and arms and shoulders and tightens her silk scarf before picking up the gift and her purse, getting out of the car, and walking down the street to the door of the friend's apartment building.

"Storytelling settings can provide a different kind of truth than a mere recitation of facts. . . . These settings can reveal the truth about what oppression did to people—not just the recitation of events, but what the oppression *felt* like, how it changed and destroyed lives, even lives not touched by a specific crime. Because so many stories can be told, a larger picture emerges in which individual victims can see their place in a community of survivors" (Teresa Godwin Phelps, quoted in Stauffer 2015).

Does storytelling keep events of the past contained there, or is it hoping to transform them into something that can accompany us into the future? Are these two opposing impulses or are they one and the same?

Does the storyteller want to remember or forget? To hang on to or let go of?

Does storytelling aim to create a utopia, to erase a dystopia, or simply to mirror one or the other?

Does the utopia come to life on the page or in the interactions between writer, reader, and text?

Is the failed attempt to tell an all-encompassing story the dystopia we want to escape? Isn't that dystopia the very essence of utopia?

What becomes of these stories in the face of the world's continuing brutalities? In the face of the monsters forever reinventing themselves?

How to stop the telling of these stories from becoming yet another piece of propaganda in the hands of this or that regime? In this or that corner of the world?

How can these stories restore our faith in our ability to rise beyond the oppressor, in our ability to create different realities? Can they even aspire to that? Can they at least restore our faith in our imaginations, remind us that they're our best tool for survivance?

And the friend buzzes them in through the sound of music and
laughter, and they open the door to a landscape woven together
from newly planted shrubs and roses and thick, tall trees whose
trunks have determined the shape and design of the walls, and the
sound of water flowing in the narrow brook made with turquoise tiles
guides them toward the entrance, the still-unfinished lobby, the
elevator, the door to the friend's apartment.
The friend takes the dessert and unwraps the gift right there and
loves the bowls and kisses her and the lover, welcoming them
inside, and as they walk into the house, she immediately falls in
love with the way it's decorated, the subtle light of candles set along
the hallway, the family pictures mounted on the wall, some black
and white, some in color, the vulnerable artworks, the old wooden
mirror with colorful glass tiles forming its frame, the drawings,
the calligraphies, the paintings, the old chest, the vase filled with
white lilies, the magazines stacked by the TV stand, the carpet,
the chandelier, the drapes, the china, the booze and sodas on the
kitchen counter, the food spread over the dining table.
They are greeted by faces that are familiar from weekly gatherings,
faces from long ago that have changed but not really, and new
faces, and they join them in recounting memories of the past

week or month or year while sipping their drinks and picking at vegetable trays and eyeing the men and women who move to house music and wonder about prospects for conversation or sex, and then someone calls out for the music to be changed to Persian pop, a request booed by some and applauded by others, and they dance to a Persian song or two and then sit down at the table for the main dishes the friend herself has cooked, and they busy themselves trying everything but she reminds the lover not to fill up because she knows there will be dessert and a homemade cake too. As she gets up to carry some dishes away to the kitchen, a woman she does not know and he does not know asks the lover about his work, and he begins to tell her about it and then asks her about hers, and she begins to tell him about it and moves her chair closer to his so she can hear better, and when she comes back from the kitchen, the lover calls her over and sits her on his lap, and the woman pauses and excuses herself to go fill her drink, and he kisses her behind the ear and moves his hand on her bare thigh, and she grabs his hand and pulls him to the entryway, away from the eyes of the others, and he slips his hand under her dress, and she places a kiss on his neck, staining his white collar with her red lipstick, and he grabs her hand and pulls her toward the room on their right, which they find is the friend's bedroom, clean and organized the way rooms in new homes are clean and organized, perfumes, foundations, eye shadows, lipsticks, blushes, hair clips decorating the vanity, a book lying half-open on the duvet, a few frames waiting to be hung up, a sliding door opening onto a small balcony, and she pushes him to the wall and slips her hand under his shirt, into his jeans, and he tries to throw her on the bed, but they hear voices approaching from the hallway, and instead they open the door to the balcony and step outside for a cigarette in the fresh night air. And beyond the balcony and the patinated bistro set and the black ashtray that is the naked body of a woman reclining and the adobe-colored flower boxes filled with pink and purple and red ice plants, she and the lover notice, in the not-so-distant distance, the prison gate and the barbed wire and the watchtowers and the hills hiding cells underneath and the faint lights and the silent winds and the highways and the overpasses and the underpasses and the lights of the cars passing through, passing through, passing through, and they decide to go back inside, to rejoin the party, but right then they notice another couple stumbling into the room, their bodies entwined, their voices morphed into hushed laughter, and the two of them choose to stay outside for a while, to sit down and smoke the hash the lover digs out from his pack of cigarettes, to be voyeurs squeezed between what's inside and what's beyond.

He takes a puff, and she takes a puff, and he gets up and begins to walk restlessly around the confined space of the balcony, and he grows more restless and stops and looks down below and then motions for her to come over to the railing, and she straightens her dress and walks to his side, careful not to make noise with her

heels, and he points down below to the neighboring lot, and she

looks but notices nothing in the darkness enfolding the land, and

he tells her to look more closely and points to a certain spot, and

she notices something moving, things moving, creatures moving,

and he looks, and she looks, and they notice horses, two horses

moving slowly in a circle, and she looks, and he looks, and they

notice a cement millstone defining the horses' movement, slow

and circular, slow and circular, as if they can't and will never stop,

as if they will never reach an end, and she looks, and he looks, and

surrounding the millstone and the horses, they notice an orchard

and a well and a small track, perhaps for the horses to exercise

their muscles, and then a junkyard of car skeletons, tires, barrels,

couches, tables, cabinets, trunks, rusted frames, tattered canvases,

and the two horses keep moving, and she and the lover choose to

stare at the two horses instead of everything else around them, and

they finish their hash holding on to one another, gasping for breath,

for air, while the couple inside laughs loudly and finds their way

out of the room and back to the party, where by now, everyone

must be busy with dessert, with the cake the friend made, and

the last tea of the night.

"Authoritarian regimes may be able to suppress organized movements or silence collective resistance. But they are limited when it comes to stifling an entire society, the mass of ordinary citizens in their daily lives" (Bayat 2010). Under such circumstances, Bayat believes everyday life and the tiniest attempts to carry on with it become "ways in which people resist, express agency, and instigate change," a form of social-political activism opposing the status quo. Bayat calls this "courage and creativity" the "art of presence."

corpse (45)
hands are fists

Corpse (7) and Corpse (8)

Age: 38 and 58
Gender: Both female
Occupation: Daycare employees
Date of Death: 25 Khordad 1388 / 15 June 2009
Place of Death: Daycare center, Tehran
Time of Death: Around 8:00 p.m.
Cause of Death: Bullets
Date of Burial: 27 Khordad 1388 / 17 June 2009
Place of Burial: Behesht-e Zahra Cemetery, Tehran

When the protests in the square end, people head to nearby streets.

Clashes break out between protesters and police and paramilitary forces in front of a Basij base.

According to some reports, the daughter and mother were headed to the Music of the Rain daycare opposite the base to do some cleaning while the school was closed and the kids weren't around.

According to other reports, the two women were members of the Basij force and were on their way home when the clashes broke out, and they went to the daycare only to take shelter there.

Once on the property, they hide behind the closed front gate.

A barrage. From above. At the walls. Through the door. They are shot.

Daughter and mother are shot in the torso and in the neck.

One side claims people were shot by forces on the roof of the base and by plainclothes agents in the crowd.

The other side claims the forces primarily used blank cartridges to disperse the crowd and replaced them with real bullets only when protesters attacked the base and set it on fire.

The head of the Tehran Basij declares that the shootings were carried out by the rioters. He refers to experts' reports and the angles of the bullet paths as evidence.

Eyewitnesses claim the people around the base were unarmed.

No official reports are provided of the specifics of the bullets found in the bodies of the daughter and the mother.

One report says the father/husband headed to the daycare after he failed to reach his daughter and wife by phone.

One witness says that after the barrage stopped, people brought a ladder, entered the property, and broke the locks on the doors. The father/husband was among them.

One report says the father/husband found the bodies of his daughter and wife together in the daycare front yard, found them covered in blood.

One report quotes another daughter saying that the three of them worked at the daycare together, that they were open that day, that they sent the last kid home around 6:15 p.m., that she decided to go home, that her sister and mother decided to stay there overnight or head home later if the clashes calmed down. She is quoted blaming the leaders of the movement for their deaths. She speaks of her sister's care for the poor, of her wish for martyrdom. She says one was shot in the head and back. The other in the head and throat.

In a picture of the daughter's head, to the right side of her neck, just under the chin, is a large hole filled with crimson tissue. Her forehead is streaked with blood.

Her head is in another woman's left hand. The woman has her hand behind her left ear. The woman wears red nail polish on her left thumb, the same red as the blood, but sparkling.

Her hair all smeared with the stickiness of insides excavated by bullets.

Over time all the color remaining in her disappears. What's left are the overwhelming streaks of blood, which continue to flow.

One witness says when the barrage stopped, faint voices could still be heard from behind the gate. Says the women were alive but died on the way to the hospital.

The father/husband is told by medical examiners that both women died immediately after the bullets hit them.

According to the brother, the sister and mother were just passing by when the attacks to the Basij base began. They took shelter in the daycare but were gunned down by the rioters. He asks, "My question to these people is: What crime did my mother and sister commit to be killed?" He demands the responsible rioters be severely punished.

Daughter and mother are buried in a two-story grave.

The grave is covered with a rug. Flowers on top. A plate of halva, decorated with pistachio. A spoon lying on the left corner.

Men and women stand around.

Men and women squat around.

Men in a semicircle at two sides of the grave. Women in a semicircle at the other two.

They say their prayers.

The gravestone carries the mother's name on top, the daughter's name below hers.

The walls of the daycare center are soon painted over to cover the bullet holes. The door to the daycare is replaced.

The two women are survived by the father/husband and at least one brother and one sister.

"Dreams are as black as death" (Adorno 2007). "Certain dream experiences lead me to believe that the individual experiences his own death as a cosmic catastrophe. . . . Our dreams are linked with each other not just because they are 'ours,' but because they form a continuum, they belong to a unified world, just as, for example, all Kafka's stories inhabit 'the same world.' The more dreams hang together or are repeated, the greater the danger that we shall be unable to distinguish between them and reality" (Adorno, quoted in Cogdde and Lonitz 2007).

Corpse (9)

Age: 25
Gender: Female
Occupation: University student majoring in literature
Date of Death: 31 Khordad 1388 / 21 June 2009
Place of Death: Keshavarz Boulevard, Tehran
Time of Death: Unknown
Cause of Death: Bullet to the neck
Date of Burial: 2 Tir 1388 / 23 June 2009
Place of Burial: Behesht-e Zahra Cemetery, Tehran

No further information available.

The information I choose to include in the narratives, is it the truth? Is it the whole truth? How do we choose? Which of the objects, the people, the voices find their way into the stories?
Why do we pick one injustice over the other?
Is having lived through this era, in this place, in this injustice justification enough for choosing to tell this story and not those of other moments and sites of oppression and repression?
Is being of this people reason enough for telling their stories and not other people's stories?
Is death the highest injustice of all?
Aren't the struggles of everyday life as important to think about and voice as these singled-out moments in history are?
Can a book aim for the stories of all, not the stories of only a few?
What is the use of the book when the dead are not coming back to life?
What can a book do for the void that has filled the life of the lover, the brother, the sister, the parents, the stranger who saw the blood bursting, who heard the sounds of the execution, who didn't see or hear directly but saw or heard in the virtual world, who didn't see or hear at all but inherited the void, dreamt the nightmare of the void?
How can the book translate the narrative of death into a narrative of life?
How can it use the language of life to translate the experience of death?
What is its use if it tells the stories of these deaths in a language other than theirs, in a context other than theirs?
What is the use of any of this while the bodies continue to decompose in plots that, in thirty years, might be shared with other, newer corpses?
How can we, as translators of these events and their narratives, find the proper language to voice them? What might the proper

language be? Is there just one? Who decides what it is? Reality? Media? Politicians? Family? Friends? Restrictions? Love? Memory? How can we translate them into the closed frame of a book, of an art form, of a report, of a memorial while celebrating the life in them? How can we accommodate a reading that constantly reopens itself, rereads itself, retranslates itself based on our distance from the event, physical and emotional, spatial and temporal, based on our relationship with the event, with the world around it, with ourselves?

How can we, within the frame of a book, keep these bodies and their voices alive, audible, relatable?

Do the wounds of their bodies and ours heal within the frame of a book that promises to hold on to the scars?

Does our healing result from the conversation coming to an end or continuing on?

How can we, within the frame of a book, anticipate and allow for all our future wounds, for the wounds of the future readers who will touch the book and be touched by it?

How can the book remain a book of journey not destination?

corpse (46)
greenness
corpse (47)
whiteness
corpse (48)
redness
corpse (49)
greenness

What is a count without a story?
What is a story without a count?
Is the count an acknowledgment?
Is the count a story in and of itself?

Who weeps for them? Who weeps for us?

corpse (53)

corpse (54)

How many deaths?
How many are enough?
Should the list include everyone? Can it?
How can a list be complete when it cannot account for the ones who disappeared without a trace, whose bodies were never turned over to the families, who have no cemetery plots or sites of memorial?
Should there even be a list if it can't be comprehensive?
How does an incomplete list make the families of the ones it has not counted feel? Do they feel betrayed?

In the small space of the gallery there are hundreds of works, hundreds of paintings, photographs, calligraphies, and sculptures, there are the voices and scents of the visitors mingling, murmuring, looking at prices or not bothering to, looking instead at other faces and bodies moving among the artworks. The water in the street gutter speeds by. The leaves are beginning to feel fall lurking. She and her friend wait for the thinking angel statue to be wrapped up. The three men wait for them outside. Soon they'll continue with the rest of their weekly gallery hopping. Someone from another group of friends repeats rumors of a soirée, another place, another event. They head to the car.

"Intellectual life—artistic life—in Mexico is very active, as are all aspects of life in Mexico. Mexico is a tremendously vital country, despite the fact that, paradoxically, it's the country where death is the most present. Perhaps being that vital is what keeps death so close" (Bolaño 2009).

They all get into her car. The friend at the wheel. She in the
front seat. The men in the back seat. The thinking angel too.
Covered in bubble wrap just to be safe, especially her wings. She
sits on the lap of one of the men. Another makes them wait as he
goes to grab something from his house a few blocks away. They sit
and watch the people going in, coming out. He comes back. Inside
the car, he reveals the already-rolled joints. Another drinks from
a plastic water bottle filled with vodka and offers it to others. Her
friend starts the car and begins to drive. She, in the
passenger seat, looks out the window.
Meandering through the streets, they pass the joint around. The
vodka too. She does not drink. She looks at the cars around them
in traffic. When they arrive at the address they were given, the
other group of friends is not yet there. They wait. The men bare the
thinking angel. Look at her. Touch her. The angel sits silently, her
wings, made from the feathers of a once-living crow, weighing on
her papier-mâché body, her long fingers poised seductively
in the air around her knees.
Others arrive. They leave the angel in the car and, with the
other group, walk toward the alley. It is almost empty. Friday
evening. Businesses closed. An old woman taking garbage out to

the garbage can, leaving some food next to it for cats. A few men idling around the corner. She wants the group to move faster, but they take their time and don't care. Introductions. Handshakes. Kisses on cheeks.

In the middle of the alley. A house. No signs. The door closed. Half metal and half glass, covered with vertical bars. Narrow. Someone rings the bell.

Someone opens the door and welcomes them in. Inside is a narrow hallway immediately slashed by a flight of floating stairs, which begins at the end of the hallway and ascends in the direction of the door, the weight of its slanting plaster soffit pushing into the newcomers' faces. Bodies move around. Someone hands her a pamphlet, the program for the night. She glances at it without really reading. A door to the right opening toward other doors opening into large and small rooms. A door at the end of the hallway leading to a balcony and a courtyard. On the right wall, a small sign that reads, "Why should we leave? Where are we going? I am staying. Come." She stares at the words. From a hidden projector, the face of a young woman appears on the soffit of the staircase, appears and disappears, comes to life only to fade again. The woman has a voice. She says things. Her features move. Her voice is silenced. She reads the sign again, "I am here to stay. Let me embrace you. Stay with me." People ascend and descend the stairs on top of her face.

"Wars, revolutions, military coups, and repressive regimes are among the circumstances that may force the formerly settled and sedate to lead picaresque and disjointed lives," pushing them to turn into wandering characters who, due to psychological, historical, and literary or aesthetic reasons, "are little inclined to see themselves as the protagonists of life stories" (Andrews 2014).

She and her friend walk into the room on the right. An installation in the middle. Boxes draped in fabric. A television on top of the boxes. A man bangs into her as he leaves the room. He doesn't say a word. She stands to one side. Ghostly words flash on the screen. The television is old. She looks at the guide in her hand. The lights are dim. She doesn't really understand the guide. Mumbling voices. A young woman's wafting perfume. She walks back to the hallway and looks for familiar faces. An old chest in the hallway that smells of aged wood, heavy with the presence of an old woman who puts things in, takes things out. She and her friend walk out to the balcony. Their feet go beyond the threshold of the hallway and the heads of the people outside suddenly turn toward them. Curious. Questions in their eyes. Suspicious. Colorful lanterns hang overhead from a clothesline. A few light bulbs shine in the trees in the garden below the balcony. She listens, tucking her scarf back away from her ear. She listens, hoping to pick up some names, some answers, find out what the place is, who the people are. Find out why they were told to come here.

I want to take her aside and talk to her, tell her some things, prepare her for the moment of revelation to come. I want to talk to her about how cities are spilling over their historical containers, becoming fluid amalgamations of the good and evil of various cities and landscapes, real and fictional, local and global, past and present and future, natural and artificial, composites of the heavens and the underworlds. I want to speak to her about how in these cities that are sites of our modern nomadic lives, those who become detectives in search of answers can only fail and arrive at more questions. And I want to say that in their failures, they are the new flaneurs of our exploded, decentered world, setting out on searches they'll dedicate their lives to, but becoming so enamored with life or drowned by waves of (hi)stories that they'll never arrive at what they intended to find. And I want to point out to her that in their loose wanderings, they come to be seen as criminals, too, displaced by the interrelations of their lives and the lives of the cities.

And I want to remind her that even so, it's all o.k., that the only thing that really matters is to keep wandering, to keep searching, to keep asking questions, to become the questions, to aim to create not a map that leads to arrival, but a map for getting lost deep in the city.

I want to embrace her and hum a calming melody in her ear, because I know, and you might know, too, that in these cities, the fates of the ones searching might not be very different from the fates of the ones they search for.

corpse (55)
sherbet to drink
flower petals
tears to shed

Corpse (10)

Age: Unknown
Gender: Male
Occupation: University student
Date of Death: 25 Khordad 1388 / 15 June 2009
Place of Death: University of Tehran dormitories,
Amirabad Street, Tehran
Time of Death: Early hours of the day
Cause of Death: Several blows to the head and neck
by electric baton
Date of Burial: 25 Khordad 1388 / 15 June 2009
Place of Burial: Behesht-e Zahra Cemetery, Tehran

In front of the gate to campus. Nighttime.
Police, special forces, paramilitary forces, plainclothes
forces.
Unrest. Slogans.
Students stand. Forces try to enter. Students throw
rocks. Forces throw rocks and tear gas.
Fire.
In the dorms, students get ready for bed.
It is illegal for police, army, and other military and
paramilitary forces to enter campus grounds. They
enter. It is unclear who ordered the entry.
Attackers in plain clothes. Students in plain clothes.
Attackers in uniform.
Fire here and there.
Everyone runs.
Someone films. Students run. Attackers curse and
beat them. In front of the library. Fires burn. Bones
break. Sounds of bullets and rocks. Tear gas. The
special forces beat students. The plainclothes forces
ask them to stop. They curse. They arrest. They call
out the names of Shiite imams. They film.

Inside the building, they break glass. They break locks. They punch holes in the doors. They have axes and daggers. They have guns. They have electric batons. They force students to lie on the floor. They touch them. To feel for knives and guns, they say. They search through possessions. They spread papers all around. They shuffle through. They break heads and hands. They stand in two lines along the hallway walls. They force students to run. To run even with broken bones. They thrust their weapons out over their shields. They beat students.

They threaten to hang. They threaten to rape.

They arrest students. Push them outside the building. Drag them on the floor. Beat them. Someone asks them to stop. They curse. They hold guns over students' heads and bodies. Someone orders them to film. To kill.

Someone calls the students spoiled. Someone orders them to lie down. Students resist. They pile students up in a corner like meat, hands and legs and heads crumpled over one another. In pajamas, bare chests, bare feet. They film the scene. They take pictures. They take students away. They beat them. Students shout and ask them to stop. They beat them. Students shout and ask why.

Some students are left there. Wounded. Unaided. Watched over so they can't get away. Left to the darkness.

Others are taken to secret detention centers. One in a basement said to belong to the interior ministry. Students are tortured. Humiliated when given water or food. Later, the links to the sources claiming documentation of the torture redirect to a page that cannot be found anymore.

Electric batons are used. Electric batons are used on heads and necks.

Students are killed. Five are confirmed dead. He is one.

No official reports on the deaths. Only the wounded are counted.

The ones who survive are handed clean clothes before they leave detention. Concerns about how they'll look when they step out.

Papers spread all around in dorm rooms and hallways. Broken chairs. Torn clothes. Bloodstains. Broken plates and cups. Bullet holes. Black ash. Torn books. Overturned beds. Overturned bookshelves. Unpaired slippers and shoes. A sticker that says "change" half torn off the door.

Students gone. Students idling. Students wondering. He and the other four students are buried secretly, without the permission or presence of their families. The families are prohibited from speaking. The families are prohibited from holding funerals.

All the data about the deaths compiled here can be found online (or, in some cases, they could be once, before they disappeared in the rabbit hole of the internet). This is not an attempt at investigative journalism; it is about using what any citizen can find, what has already been made available, by sources from both sides, journalists, citizen journalists, human rights organizations, families, friends, and others, in the form of texts, videos, audio files, photographs, et cetera. It's about being curious, wanting to know, and setting out on the journey of the search.

Re: the questions.

The ability or failure to ask questions about things that exist, have existed, things that happen, have happened, about their truth, has "something to do with the ability to make and hear cries for help. . . . Questions and their assumed interlocutors thus open up a whole world beyond curiosity and research, leading us fairly directly to conditions necessary for human beings inhabiting a shared world" (Stauffer 2015, discussing Emmanuel Levinas). "Research takes form as a question, and a question addresses itself to others. That is an existential as much as an ethical truth" (Stauffer 2015).

Questions are there from the very beginning. They prompt the search; they prompt the writing. And they shall remain until the very end, even beyond. Though they will change and new questions will keep being born throughout the process. As if each page is a layer removed, a layer closer to the core, though not necessarily leading to anything.

It is only by way of questions that the text can be transformed into a body that offers its wounds for examination and treatment, opening itself up and inviting the writer and readers into its vulnerability and fragility.

Without the questions, the book would become a manual and a postcard, a goddess posing for cameras, too pleased with her limbs and her arms, with her words and her voice. It might imagine itself as the authoritative text, the representative text, the text that will leave its mark on the literary landscape of this place and time. Failing to bare its gaps and failures to readers, growing too sure of itself, a closed text will suffer illusions of grandeur, will mimic the very forces it has set forth to expose and oppose.

"I don't know which is the real life except that the dream life is of course the most real" (Cixous 1993).

"That frontier between the unconscious and preconscious—the frontier of dreaming—is the metaphorical place of that distinctively human conversation with ourselves in which raw experience that simply is-what-it-is . . . is transformed into experience that has accrued to itself a modicum of the quality of 'I-ness'" (Ogden 2001). "The internal conversation known as dreaming is no more an event limited to the hours of sleep than the existence of stars is limited to the hours of darkness. Stars become visible at night when their luminosity is no longer concealed by the glare of the sun. Similarly, the conversation with ourselves that in sleep we experience as dreaming continues unabated and undiluted in our waking life" (Ogden 2001).

corpse (56)
hushed ceremonies
prayers
videos

The people on the balcony are smoking. A round copper tray of now-empty tea glasses and a light-green crystal bowl of sugar cubes are on the table, which is the cut trunk of a once-living tree. Silence suddenly, as if their presence, now too long, is an intrusion. They walk back in, up the stairs. Rooms in front and to the right. A crowd waiting to come down the stairs. A woman hands her an envelope. The silent words of the face projected on the staircase reverberate in her head: Where are you going? Come. She steps into the room to the right. Seats in profile. Rows and rows. A few people sit and watch something on the far-right wall. She looks. A journey. A train moving on the wall. The doors of a train car opening and closing. Music. People look her up and down. She sits down, constantly turning her attention from the video to the door and the people coming in or leaving in the middle of the short film that plays on repeat. Some sit on the floor. The scent of incense permeates the room. She steps into the train car. Sits in front of a stranger. The train speeds out of a station. They stare into one another. The man wears the beard of an intellectual or an artist. The train moves into a tunnel, and she becomes the ghost of a burlesque dancer reflected on the window behind her, and he becomes the ghost of a sculptor reflected on the window

behind him, and the train moves forward in the darkness of the

tunnel, and she dances, and he chisels, and she touches him, and

he touches her, and they breathe in one another, away from the

eyes of the audience, and when the train comes out on the other

side, the ghosts of the dancer and the sculptor have separated and

disappeared, but their footprints remain on the windows, and she

and the man are still sitting, staring into and beyond the

windows and each other.

The train arrives at a station. She leaves the train car. She leaves

the room. Gives her seat to a young man.

She clutches the letter she has been handed. Puts it in her purse.

She walks through the door of another room. An old man wearing

pajamas sits in a faded burgundy armchair by the door as if he

were a wax figure guarding the entrance. Staring into an unknown

reality beyond him or trapped forever in the clock and the books

and the candleholders on the shelf before him. A cat mews and

moves around the feet of his chair. An alarm clock sounds. She

hesitates for a moment, wondering if the room is off-limits, but

sees others sitting on the couch on the far side. She mumbles a

hello to the old man and hesitantly steps in. On the side table,

several newspapers. On the coffee table, dozens of envelopes. All

similar to the one she has just put into her purse. A woman picks one

randomly and asks her if she wants it. She reaches into her purse.

Her envelope is still there. She shakes her head no. Someone laughs downstairs in the courtyard. A man gets up from a chair in front of a laptop and hands the headphones to another man who has been waiting behind him. He gets up. He sits down. A video she cannot see runs on the laptop screen. She turns around and glances at the old man. His cigarette ash falls into the crystal ashtray on the arm of the chair. The cat jumps on his lap. In another corner of the room, suitcases piled on top of one another up to the ceiling. Old. Heavy. Dozens. A few scattered around. She goes and stands next to them. Looks inside one that is open on the floor. Clothes. Photo albums. Books. A few personal items. A woman brings in more items and sits by the suitcase. Small bags of roasted nuts and sweets. A few clay figurines. A folded map. More books and photo albums. More personal items. She puts a few things in, takes a few out, rearranges others. She opens the albums and leafs through. Takes a few photographs out of one. Tears a few. Puts kisses on one. Throws the album aside. Puts the photos she took out in a folder and places it in the pocket of the suitcase. A few handwritten notes too. The map too. She goes through the books. She reads titles. Smells pages. Reads a few words. She takes a few pieces of clothing out. She puts a few more books in. The cat moves among the clothes, jumps inside the suitcase, lies comfortably over the woman's life, as if to safeguard the objects from being devoured by the suitcase. The cat mews constantly. She stares at the cat. She stares at the figurines still lying on the floor outside the suitcase. A mother and child. A thinking angel. Covered with bubble wrap. For protection. To keep from breaking. She puts them inside the suitcase. The cat rearranges its body. She stares at the cat, at the clothes, the albums, the books, the figurines. The old man smokes his cigarette. The old man doesn't look at her or the cat. Someone comes in with a tray of cold water. The woman packing takes a glass. The cat jumps out of the suitcase and follows the woman with the tray out of the room. She drinks the water. Takes everything out of the suitcase. Arranges everything patiently next to the wall of suitcases. She crawls into the suitcase. In the shape of a fetus, she fits in its confines. A man walks toward her and the suitcase. He crouches down. He halfway closes the top. The column of suitcases piled on top of one another suddenly crumbles. The suitcases open from inside. One after another. A man, a woman, a child, a cat, a woman, a child, a man, a woman, a woman, an angel, a mother, a child, a woman, an angel step out of them. One after another. They all gather around the half-closed suitcase next to the man and the woman. The cat comes back to the room, finds its way to the suitcase, striding through the objects nearby, the figurines left behind, the bodies amassing. The cat scratches the suitcase. As if to mark it. To sanctify it. The bodies sit cross-legged in a circle on the carpet and keep vigil around the suitcase embracing the fetus woman. Still standing to the side, she hears them humming.

The language unknown. She wonders whether she should sit
down and join in.

Someone puts a hand on her shoulder. She turns around. Her
friend looks at her and points to the large television a few steps
away. "I have been long gone but I am caged here forever," read the
words endlessly repeating on the screen. She pauses. She stares.
He invites her out to the courtyard for a cigarette. She follows him
from the room. The old man coughs. The singing continues.
A woman standing like a statue asks if she has an envelope. She
nods yes. The woman asks if she wants another envelope.
She shakes her head no and walks downstairs.

"We're reasonable human beings . . . , not spirits out of a manual of magic realism, not postcards for foreign consumption and abject masquerade. In other words, we're beings who have the historic chance of opting for freedom, and also—paradoxically—life" (Bolaño 2011).

As she passes the chest in the hallway, she notices an old off-white engagement dress hanging inside staring at her. She smells the scent of bodies aroused. She smells rosewater. She walks out. On the balcony, the tree-trunk seats are all occupied. She walks down the stairs toward the small garden and trees. A lemon tree. A sour cherry tree. Rosebushes. Her friends are hanging around and chatting. An old woman holds up a basket for a man picking sour cherries on top of a ladder. The woman wears the engagement dress, torn to shreds. The man is naked except for military boots and a turban. There are no sour cherries on the tree. The scent of lemon rising through the soil's pores. Rosebuds climbing up the tree. Birds hanged by their necks, dancing in between the branches as if caressed by the fingers of an imaginary wind. A few people sitting on the tiled stairs, passing around black-and-white photographs, murmuring, laughing out loud. She notices another staircase. She counts thirteen steps. Farther down. Into a basement. She leaves her friends and descends the stairs.

"Bring your bodies to our bodies and together we will become new bodies" (Borzutzky 2015).

of flag and of hope

What makes a narrator? A fair narrator?
How many narrators should there be? Could there be?
How can I be a narrator? A fair narrator?
How can I channel the voices of the dead, of the living?
How can I bear the brutality, the intimacy, the immediacy, of a moment, of a place?
How can I be a medium while lost in the search, in the labyrinthine hell of humanity and history?
Am I writing these lives to give voice to them, or to give myself a voice and a body?
Is this an attempt to go from numbness to feeling? From dried eyes to tears?
What if we can't cry? What if we don't?
Have the dead surrendered? Have we? Have I?
Who is listening?
Who cares?
Why do they care? Why do they listen? What will they do with these stories?
Does my speaking pose a threat to me as the speaker? To the subjects, living and dead?
Does reading these stories pose a threat to the readers?
What are the risks?
How to narrate what some in power want forgotten? What others in power want remembered only for their own agendas?
Will the narratives serve the bodies and the memories?
Will they serve the living, the surviving?
What if they harm them?
Can the writing and reading of these lives and deaths create a community of mourners? Can the mourners breathe life back into the dead and the living? Into me? Into you? What would this look like?
What about the genes that carry the trauma: on and on and on?
Will the trauma ever stop being inherited?
Will humans ever change? Will the chain of evil ever be broken?

black of mourning

A ceremony. A ritual. On the night before completion, presentation, defense.
An altar. Turquoise. The manuscript. Images. Of the homeland. The land of the living and the dead. The black-and-white girl staring back. Family lineage. Mutilated women of the desert. Poetry the nation goes to for divination. Soil of the land. The dessert of the dead. Bracelets. Incense. Candles. Mirror. Prayers. Water. The hoopoe.
A wake. A vigil. A reading. Of the living. A recitation. Of the dead. All of them. All of it. An embodiment. All night long. Out loud. To be spoken. To be heard. Permission asked. Of the living and the dead. Voices. Tears. All together in flight. Ululation. Union. The passage. Granted. Only then, the reflection in the water.

bodies falling
bodies lying
bodies carried
bodies buried

"I can't help but think, forever, about absorption. About what it means to be absorbed. About how a community, a city, a country, a nation, absorbs, or refuses to absorb, its bodies, its ghosts, its citizens" (Borzutzky 2015).

"A writing of absorption. A writing of envelopment. Of dissolution, evaporation. / Because everywhere there are people with no voice who cannot be absorbed. / Because there are things like this, because there are unabsorbed bodies, writing continues to take place" (Borzutzky 2015).

The door is half-open. A dim light is on. Shadows move around inside. She opens the door. Sneaks in. Small figurines sit around a table, drinking and smoking and talking and dancing and laughing and crying and coming, all on the narrow wooden bed that is their stage, and their shadows grow larger and larger on the wall. Underneath the bed, she notices several white shrouds, wrapped as if around corpses or statues or bundles of discarded clothing or objects. A heap of soil piled close by, as if dug out of a trench or a grave. A compass lying to one side of the patch of soil. She stands there at the door and watches for a while. She hears them but does not understand them. A sign next to the light switch reads, "Lost Beings. Welcome to the party." The sound of a fountain rises from the soil. The soil remains dry and cracked. A voice from a hidden loudspeaker asks, where are you going? I am staying. We are all staying. Where are you? We are all here. I am here. Let me take you. Come. Come. Breathe. Get lost with me. In me. Stay. Come. The party goes on. The party ignores her presence. The water begins to flow. The shrouds begin to rearrange themselves under the bed. The soil disappears. The voice continues to speak, where are you? Where are you? She hears her friends calling her name. She stands there, frozen, watching the figurines.

"Some say you have no right to talk about the dead. So I talk of them as living, their bodies standing in the street's bend" (Scenters-Zapico 2015).

Her friend puts a hand on her shoulder, guides her out of the basement. She runs her hand through her hair and adjusts her scarf. Her hair is covered with soil. He offers her a half-smoked cigarette. She takes it. Others join them. Another friend offers her a joint. She takes it. She hears a scream in the basement. The birds hanged by their necks begin to sing in the tree branches. The lights go off in the basement. She wants to go back. Her friends tell her it's time to leave. Her friends pull her along. Out through the courtyard, through the hallway, through the door with the metal bars.

I am glad her friends are there to look out for her, guide her back from the basement, lead her away. She'll need them as we near the end. Or the beginning.

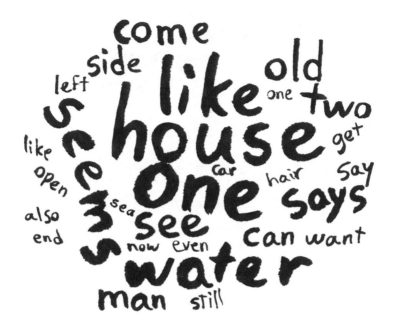

"Sleep and dreams occur in the plane of the imagination (*hadrat al-khayal*) and must be subject to interpretation" (El Shakry 2018, discussing Ibn Arabi).

"The dilemma is 'whether to believe or to interpret one's dream'" (Jean-Michel Hirt, according to El Shakry 2018).

"Dreams, like texts, had both manifest (*zahir*) and latent (*batin*) meanings. The latent meanings of dreams could be understood with the help of signs (*ayat*) and allusions (*isharat*)" (El Shakry 2018).

Corpse (11)

Age: 61
Gender: Male
Occupation: Infectious diseases specialist, head of the infectious diseases clinic at Imam Khomeini Hospital, associate professor at the University of Tehran
Date of Death: 30 Shahrivar 1389 / 21 September 2010
Place of Death: Keshavarz Boulevard, Tehran
Time of Death: Between 8:00 p.m. and 9:00 p.m.
Cause of Death: Assassination
Date of Burial: 3 Mehr 1389 / 25 September 2010
Place of Burial: Behesht-e Zahra Cemetery, Tehran

He leaves his office after work.
Tomorrow he's leaving the country to visit his youngest son, who lives in the u.s.
As he is getting into his car, he is shot at by four men on two motorbikes.
Two bullets. One hits the door of his car. The other pierces the side of his torso.
He dies next to his car, in front of his office.
The bullet shells are never found.
His personal belongings, including his wedding ring, disappear when his body is transferred to the medical examiner's office. They are never returned to his family.
He doesn't make it to his son.
The son gets a phone call. He learns of a delay, of an accident, and finally of the truth.
The doctor had examined the bodies of some of the torture victims from the infamous Kahrizak Detention Center.

He was under pressure to state that the tortured prisoners had died of meningitis. He refused, his sons say.

He had also examined former prisoners who suffered from urinary and genital infections. He was ordered to state that their infections were caused by meningitis. He refused.

He spoke once to foreign media about the prisoners' infections.

He gradually became burdened and depressed.

He spoke once or twice to his sons about the rape and torture of the prisoners.

Eyewitnesses say the shooters hung around in the neighborhood for a while, waiting for the doctor to leave his office.

Eyewitnesses speak of a cab that blocked the doctor's car.

The shooters did not wear masks or helmets.

The shooters used silencers.

Eyewitnesses provide facial composites to the police. The sketches are never referred to or analyzed.

According to some reports, an eyewitness who went to the police station to offer a facial composite was turned away.

The family demands an investigation.

The family demands that images from traffic cameras be studied.

They never are.

The family is told the cameras were malfunctioning at the time.

The family contacts the health minister regarding the case. The minister promises to follow up on the case with the Ministry of Information.

The police chief denies any connection between the assassination and the doctor's examination of the bodies from the infamous detention center, which was ultimately shut down. The family is informed that the assassination was carried out for personal motives.

None of the doctor's colleagues believe this scenario. No evidence is found of the doctor having had any personal issues with anyone. The sons speak of the father's warm relationship with his students, of his love for his patients, of the patients' love and respect for the father, of the father's generosity, of the time he lent a large sum of money to a patient in need. When his death is announced on the university's website, many former patients and students show respect and offer condolences in the comments section.

Immediately after the shooting, dozens of police officers and government officials arrive on the scene. It's as if this had been organized beforehand. The sons wonder about this. The officials film the scene of the incident. The films are never referred to.

The father's office is sealed off for several months. The family is not allowed access to his belongings. They are not informed whether any evidence is found there, whether anything is confiscated.

Images from the CCTVs for the office and the neighboring drugstore are collected. They are never analyzed.

The family is told the police and judiciary offices have terminated the investigation. They are told the case has been resolved, closed, and archived. Despite the family's multiple inquiries, they are never informed of the results of the investigation. The sons believe the manner in which the assassination was carried out proves the shooters were backed by men in power. The sons believe men in power feared their father would reveal the secrets of the prison once he was out of the country.

The sons believe their father died because he did not agree to lie.

Due to the complications of the case and visa concerns, the son living in the u.s. is not able to attend the father's funeral.

The doctor is the second doctor involved with the examination of victims from the detention center who has died under suspicious circumstances.

The doctor is survived by his wife, his sons, and a daughter.

corpse (57)

Corpse (12)

Age: 22
Gender: Male
Occupation: Laborer
Date of Death: 15 Mordad 1388 / 6 August 2009
Place of Death: Tehran
Time of Death: Unknown
Cause of Death: Blunt-force injuries
Date of Burial: 17 Mordad 1388 / 8 August 2009
Place of Burial: Behesht-e Zahra Cemetery, Tehran

He is not political. But he participates in the protests after the election.
One night he does not come home. The mother stays awake, worried.
The family starts to search. To no avail.
They receive a call seven days later.
Someone informs them of his arrest. No further information.
The family continues to search. To no avail.
A few days later two plainclothes agents show up at their house. Search the house. The son's belongings. They inform them of his arrest. Provide no further information.
A few days later the family spots his name on the list of prisoners held at Evin Prison. They go to court. They are informed their son can be released on bail. The father provides the bail.
He was transferred to Evin just two days prior to his release. The family never finds out about his whereabouts before Evin.
He has grown burdened and silent.
Bruises on his face. Bruises around his waist. Severe pain in his sides and kidneys.

He does not recount what happened to him. Does not want to worry the family.

He speaks only of being blindfolded. Of being forced to confess. Of beatings. Of one potato and one piece of bread for dinner every night.

He screams. During nightmares.

He fears everyone and everything. Fears being watched and followed.

His two sisters try to cheer him up.

His mother kisses his cheeks.

His mother reminds him that she warned him. Not to go. Not to get involved.

He says everyone was going. He says he was just one of many.

Ten days after his release, he goes out.

The family receives a call, giving them news.

He fainted in the street. Became unconscious. Was transferred to a hospital by strangers. The family rushes to the hospital.

He has fallen into a coma.

Both his kidneys have failed. He undergoes dialysis.

His lungs are infected.

His two sisters become his nurses.

A doctor mentions to the father that the condition of the kidneys is caused by severe beatings.

Twenty-four days after he is hospitalized, he dies.

The hospital registers the cause of death as unknown.

The family is asked if they have any complaints.

The family remains silent for fear of not receiving the body. They say not now. They say they will follow up later, when they're in better condition.

The family receives the body two days after the death.

The family buries the son in the upper level of their elder son's grave.

After the seventh day of mourning, the family files a complaint. They are told the case is already closed. The family hires a lawyer. They receive no answers.

The family registers their son's name with the committee the defeated camp has set up to identify the victims of protest violence. Their son becomes one of the many on the list. Twenty days after his death.

A national TV reporter goes to the grave. Shows the name of the elder son as proof that the son the family speaks of having lost has actually died many years ago. He films the small temporary sign with the name of the younger son. He says the sign is not the kind provided by the cemetery, that the family has made it themselves, that it is a lie.

The family receives calls from family and friends, questioning, wondering, wanting to know the truth. The family has to convince them of their son's death.

A blog belonging to a person with the same name is updated. The author writes that he is surprised by the news of the death, his own death. The author is interviewed. He announces that he is alive, that the news of his death was a sham.

News agencies aligned with the regime repeat the suspicions, raising questions about the death.

The mother speaks of the son's friends having filmed his body being washed and prepared for burial in the morgue.

The father fears for his son's body. He fears it will be exhumed and sequestered to cover up the death. He sits at the grave from dawn to dusk, when he is forced to leave the cemetery for the night. This is his routine for several days.

The bail deed remains with the court even after the son's death.

The lawyer files a complaint against the national TV. The complaint is disregarded.

The lawyer tries to file a complaint against the blogger. The court in charge of cyber crimes rejects the complaint.

The mother wonders how the blogger can question the life and death of another just because they share a name. Whether they truly share a name.

The mother says the denial of the death is an extra burden to carry.

The mother speaks of the sympathy of the people, of their calling the son a martyr, of how much it all means to them.

The mother speaks of the burden of seeing the lawyer in charge of their case and other similar ones taken away from her children and imprisoned. The mother wishes she were imprisoned instead. Wants to see the lawyer released and back with her family, her young children.

The family demands an official copy of the report from the medical examiner's office.

They don't receive one until eight months later. No mention of the kidney failure, of the lung infection. The official cause of death is stated as poisoning.

The family wants to follow up. The judge rejects their inquiries.

The case is closed.

The mother speaks of the pain growing more acute with each day that passes.

The family fears holding a ceremony for their son's death anniversary. They ask people to just remember him, light a candle in remembrance.

They gather at his grave. The police are present. Clashes. Arrests.

The mother mentions a young woman who was loved by their son. The woman remembers him.

The woman stays by the family's side. The woman invokes his name to survive the loss, to pass her university exams. The mother knows her suffering. The family loves the woman.

The family believes the revenge of their son and of the other young men and women remains in the hands of God.

What Is that unknown force larger than us that encourages us
to go on?
What is that faith?
Faith in God? What is the role of God in all this?
"This book is not a book. / It's not a song. / Or a poem. Or
thoughts. / But tears, pain, weeping, despair that cannot yet be
stopped or reasoned with. Political fury strong like one's faith
in God. Even stronger than that. More dangerous because it is
endless" (Duras 2011).
Fury? What is the role of fury in all this?
And love? What is the role of love?
What happened to the lovers? To the absence in their arms, their
bodies, their mouths?
Where are the lovers? Where are they in these narratives? Are
their bodies, their voices, their views censored? By parents, by
authorities, by themselves?
And the land? What is the role of the land in all this? The
fatherland, the motherland, the homeland?
How do the dead redefine the homeland? What about the
survivors? Their silences, their screams? How do they redefine
the homeland?
What becomes of the homeland? Does it embrace or reject its
traumas?
What lullabies will it sing to its unborn children?
What lullabies will it sing to the lovers?

room
water
house
one
seems
like

The text of the dreams is transferred from a handwritten notebook to a Word document. The text is simultaneously translated from Persian to English if necessary. It amounts to 155 dream entries, 35,000 words.

Some of the dreams are documented with the utmost attention to detail. Others include only a few key words, jotted down first thing in the morning in the hopes that they would conjure the dreams later, when they could be written down in whole. These dreams were usually lost forever before they could be documented.

Then they are translated anew: the text in a Word document becomes text in a word cloud. The circles of words are the dream world distilled. They decode the themes of the dreams, the struggles of the unconscious in the aftermath of the events, manipulating an unconscious that is already displaced in geography and lifestyle and language, an unconscious that is already altered in the remembrance, documentation, and multiple translations of the dreams.

In the alley, her friends sit her down on the curb and tell her to wait and breathe while they go to the store around the corner for water and provisions for the gathering later that night. She suddenly remembers the envelope. She digs into her purse and pulls it out, then looks around before opening it. She notices the girl she followed from the bus lingering near the door to the gallery, holding an armful of narcissus, begging visitors to buy just one bouquet, one bouquet, please, or five for a discount, or take them all for your girlfriend, she'll love you so much, and I'll be able to go home for the night, please, just one bouquet. The girl sees her on the curb. She walks toward her. Hesitantly. Pauses. Looks around. Walks faster. Looks around. Sits down next to her and puts the flowers on the ground. She digs into her satchel, brings out a folded newspaper, hands it to her. She glances at the paper in her hand. None of the headlines catch her eye. Something falls onto her lap from between the pages. An envelope. Exactly like the one she was handed at the gallery, the one she just put back in her purse, unopened, unread. She turns toward the girl. The girl is not there. The flowers are. She looks up and around. The girl has disappeared. She has left her narcissus behind. All of them. She opens the envelope. A handwritten note in the style of a newspaper article: a headline, a column.

"Bank Manager and Art Dealer Found Dead."

She reads on. The bank's basement. A corpse. An empty bottle of cyanide pills in his hand. No will. No note left behind for the family. His vomit dried around his mouth. Prayer beads and two cell phones by his side. An electrician went down to fix the wires. He found the body. Several days later. The body disfigured and blown up. The body was buried in silence. No funeral. No ceremonies. No investigation followed.

I want to delay this forever for her, let her go on with her search for the other bodies, but I know she has been safeguarding herself for too long, that it's not for the best, this illusion of safety, this ignorance, this detachment, this hiding in a merely intellectual endeavor. The hiding only goes so far.

Even her dreams are dissolving, becoming more and more haunting, trying to tell her something.

I need the story to lead her away from the statues and toward the other bodies. I need her to meet the other woman. Once again. The other woman will help her cross the threshold.

one body against another
one body attacked by many
one body praised by many
one body beside another

Nations as bodies. Languages as bodies. I hold on to those of the
mother and the father. Adopt others.

What does the choice of one language over another mean for the
translation of these (hi)stories into the space of the book?

How do these events, narrated in a book in English, compare to
those narrated in a Persian one? What does it mean to write them
originally in English rather than write them in Persian, then translate
them into English? How can they be "originally" written in English
when their sources were in Persian, when I experienced them in
Persian, when their reality was Persian?

How can the narratives be faithful?

Should they be faithful to the original event or to the text of the
event? Whose version?

Shouldn't they be faithful simply to the world of the story?

What is faithfulness?

What is translation?

How can one translate an original through one's own body to
create a new original that is of the event, of the text, of the self,
of the Other?

What do the multiple layers of translation do to help these lives and
these bodies continue to breathe? Can breathing be translated into
words, or can it be truly sensed only in the white spaces between
and around and within the words?

one body
one body
two bodies

corpse (58)

corpse (72)

corpse (80)

corpse ( )

corpse
corpse
corpses

corpses
corpses
corpses

She grabs the other envelope from her purse and opens it. There is a map and a note inside. The note is written in the same handwriting:

"Meet me tomorrow at noon. The teahouse."

Corpse (13)

Age: 34
Gender: Female
Date of Death: 6 Dey 1388 / 27 December 2009
Place of Death: Vali-e Asr Square, Tehran
Time of Death: Unknown
Cause of Death: Run over by a vehicle
Date of Burial: 23 Dey 1388 / 13 January 2010
Place of Burial: Behesht-e Zahra Cemetery, Tehran

A single mother.
Goes out to get nazri food for lunch. Like many others in town. On the Day of Ashura.
Protests are taking place.
Chaos.
A police truck hits her, backs up, goes forward again, twice crushing her body under the wheels.
Her head.
Blood.
Green shirt under her manteau.
Her arms.
White shoes. Crushed legs.
A woman screams.
A man says something about a car. Smashing her.
A man curses.
A man says something about a car. That they can use to take her to the hospital.
A clinic or a hospital. A crowd of people. Shouts.
God is great. Shouts. Calling on Imam Hussein.
People gather around the car. People help with her body, film with their cell phones, chant slogans.
Death to the dictator.
My martyr sister, we will continue on your path.

Several people, including a man in a white medical-staff uniform, struggle to move the body.

A man asks a woman to step back so he can help with the body.

A woman asks for the sheets to be removed from the face so she can film her.

A woman cries. A woman screams.

Blood on her face.

Her hair disheveled.

Her eyes closed.

When she does not return home, a friend asks around. Hears about a woman matching her description being hit. Checks with the neighborhood police station. Learns it was her friend. Goes to the friend's mother's to inform her.

The mother cannot find the daughter in hospitals, anywhere. Seventeen days later. She receives a call. Finds her in the morgue of a detention center.

The body bloated. Crushed. Bruised. Rotten. Her face disfigured.

Official cause of death stated as collision with a hard object. Object unidentified.

The mother wants to know. Hears the eyewitnesses' accounts.

The mother goes to the police. Goes to court. Opens a case. Wants to know. She is accused of lying. She is asked to bring in evidence of the killing. She is asked to provide names of the killers.

She is offered blood money. She rejects the blood money. Says she might have raised her with empty hands, with hard work, that they might have nothing, but that she will not exchange her daughter's blood for money. She only wants the culprits to be identified.

Eventually, she stops going to court.

The mother calls her late daughter a freedom fighter, a nationalist. Says she loved to travel around the country. Says she had just signed up for a carpet weaving class. Says she is a martyr of the people. The mother is thankful for the people, says they have witnessed and will never forget. The mother says her daughter's revenge is in the hands of God. The mother takes in her daughter's daughter.

The daughter is six at the time of her mother's death. She becomes depressed. She screams. She does not like to go to school. Asks for her mother. Wants her to come back home. Her grandmother tells her that her mother has gone to heaven. She stares at her grandmother with pained eyes, says heaven is far, far away.

She is survived by her mother and daughter.

The woman I resurrect, is she the one you resurrect? The one she will resurrect? If they are not one and the same, how will they meet? Where will they meet? Can they?

of birth
of death
of birth
of death
of birth

of birth
of death
of death
of death
of birth

Are we worthy of death?
Are we capable of life?

the numbers are a mystery

Dreams belong to a world still immune. A world that the men in power, those who surveil and censor, cannot yet touch, understand, control. A reminder that despite everything, there are still parts of ourselves that they cannot regulate or redact.

Voluntarily sharing this last private space, allowing entry into the mystery that is still inaccessible even to scientists, even to myself, makes me vulnerable; but could it also, paradoxically, make me powerful? Am I, with this gesture, showing that I am not afraid to bare what is most intimate, what is most private, what even I myself fail to understand?

Dreams must be spoken and included in these (hi)stories— of mine, of ours, of hers, of theirs—because they are our most autonomous creation. A reminder that no matter how hard they try, and no matter how hard we try, we will continue to translate and write our lives, in languages neither they nor we can fully understand. This is our power. Our dreams are "a theatre in which the dreamer himself is the scene, the player, the prompter, the producer, the author, the public, and the critic" (Jung 2010). It is I, not even the conscious I, but the ancient, unknowable, unconscious one, who, in conversation with the totality of my being, is the sole creator of my dreams. Whatever happens out there, she is still directing the dreams, dreams that do not just recite pasts but also prophesize futures. Dreams are maps that forever write and translate themselves, guiding us into and away from ourselves.

She arrives early to the meeting. She walks around the square.
Eyes once again looking her up and down. The same ones. Different
ones. She lingers for a while by the same newsstand, buying a
magazine and two of the day's newspapers. The salesman is not
the one from the previous time, but he looks at her as though he
recognizes her. Instead of her change, he gives her a pack of tissues.
She looks at her watch and walks to the teahouse. The doors and
windows are all open. She calls out to the waiter, who is at the door
rinsing tea glasses with boiling water and pouring the water out on
the pavement. She asks him for a table. Unsure. In a low voice. He
looks at her, looks inside, looks back at her. Looking. As if she
were out of her mind. Not saying a word.
She peeks inside. The customers are all men, sitting around the
white plastic tables, drinking tea, smoking hookahs, laughing out
loud or holding discussions in hushed voices. Men who look like
truck drivers taking a break from the road, like hardworking day
laborers, like rogues or dealers, men with the tanned, rough faces
of men of the street, their two-day beards making them look older,
more tired, their mustaches, short or long, defining them, ensuring
they belong to this place, this time. Pinned to the peeling walls are

old, faded posters of landscapes, and in the middle, a large image
of a religious figure she can't recognize.

She looks back at the waiter and notices two empty tables. She
is hesitant but asks again for one. He looks at her, murmuring
something she doesn't catch under his breath, walks out, and
begins giving her directions to a proper-for-a-woman café around
the corner on the main street. She looks back at him and repeats
her request, this time in a louder voice. She looks around and
says she wants to see the manager.

He is stunned. His mouth hangs open. His eyes search inside the
teahouse. His cleaning cloth is suspended between his fingers.
Looking offended, he walks inside, toward a man busy solving a
puzzle while sipping tea and puffing at his hookah. The two talk,
and the man glances at her and says something to the waiter, and
the waiter nods and goes to a corner table by the window, farthest
from the crowd, and starts cleaning it up. He glances at her every
few seconds while he rubs the table clean, rubbing hard as if he
wants to skin it. Finally, he comes back out and calls her in. There
is no malice or even disapproval in his eyes or his voice.
Just questions. He ushers her to the table.

As she sits and orders tea, he can no longer stop himself and
reminds her again that there is a more proper place with better tea
and food just around the corner. She looks at him and instead of
answering she asks him whether he would serve her a hookah. He

doesn't even bother to answer and walks away. She watches him as he works at the big samovar in a corner by the manager's desk, piles of glasses and saucers sitting to one side, and listens to the bubbling sound of the water in the hookahs. He comes back with a tea glass on a saucer and a little tin of sugar cubes. He leaves them on the table, and as he walks away, he explains to her that the tea will take awhile to brew, as if he wants her to know she'll be sitting there, waiting, all by herself in their crowd when she could have just walked around the corner to the more proper place for a woman. She puts her magazine and newspapers on the table and begins to read. She can't really concentrate, even though the men don't really seem to mind her after the initial shock of her presence. It's as if she has become invisible, sitting at the corner table by the window, pretending to read as she waits for the woman who sent her the map and the message.

house One

"*It is the feeling of secret* we become acquainted with when we dream, that is what makes us both enjoy and at the same time fear dreaming. When you are possessed by a dream, . . . you possess the unknown secret. It is this, not the possibility of knowing the secret, that makes you both dream and write: the beating presence of it, its feeling" (Cixous 1993).

wounds
scars

She arrives late. Before she even settles in her seat, she has waved the waiter over. Instead of the ragged veil, she wears a short manteau and a colorful cotton scarf, but her eyes have the same strange, familiar sparkle. She looks younger and yet older than the woman she followed the other day, if such a thing is possible. Approaching with a fresh teapot and a plate of halva, the waiter greets her warmly, as if he knows her, as if she belongs and is welcomed. She pours tea for the two of them, reaches into one of the shopping bags she has put on the chair next to hers, brings out newspapers, and sets them on the table. They sip their tea. Neither speaks.

She takes one last gulp of her tea.

I have to leave now.

Who are you?

She takes a bite of the halva, reaches into her purse, tucks several bills under the fresh teapot, and rises from her chair.

You should have some halva, say a prayer.

She grabs her bags, rearranges her scarf, begins to walk away.

Your newspapers.

She turns around, half sits down again.

When I was born, I was given the birth certificate of an older sister who had died a few months before. Perhaps my parents had decided I was to replace her, or perhaps it was just the easier, cheaper solution. With the borrowed birth certificate came a borrowed official name. I don't know if I became a vessel for the life of the one who had died, so she could continue to live through me, or if I imposed my own life on her name, her identity, her being, she says in a low voice, then pauses and takes a deep breath before putting her right hand on the papers and pushing them toward her.

And then she gets up without saying a word, in a rush, as if she has to be somewhere, has to leave before it's too late, nodding good-bye to her, chatting with the waiter for a second, waving to the manager, and walking out, leaving her there by herself, with the newspapers.

What will happen to her when she turns the page and faces what
she has known all along, has been living all along, but has struggled
to keep at a distance? What will happen when she feels the weight
of her life and the lives and deaths of others in the weight of the
words on the page entering her like never before? The way it has
entered you and me? What will happen when she becomes the
reader of these pages she has been a part of all along?
Can I, can anyone, go on protecting her?
What will become of her, of me, of us, of them, of you?

"I am leaving—says death without adding that he's taking me along" (Lispector 2012).

She pulls the newspapers toward her. There's something hard between the pages. She leafs through them and comes to a dossier hidden inside. There is a note on the cover in a handwriting that she's come to know. It reads, "You've been following the wrong bodies. The bodies you want are in here."

Bibliography

Adorno, Theodor W. Epigraph to *Dream Notes*. Edited by Christoph Gödde and Henri Lonitz. Translated by Rodney Livingstone. Malden, MA: Polity Press, 2007.

Agamben, Giorgio. *Remnants of Auschwitz: The Witness and the Archive*. Translated by Daniel Heller-Roazen. New York: Zone, 2002.

Andrews, Chris. *Roberto Bolaño's Fiction: An Expanding Universe*. New York: Columbia University Press, 2014.

Bayat, Asef. *Life as Politics: How Ordinary People Change the Middle East*. Stanford, CA: Stanford University Press, 2010.

Bolaño, Roberto. "Godzilla in Mexico." In *The Romantic Dogs: 1980–1998*. Translated by Laura Healy. New York: New Directions, 2008.

———. "The Lost." In *Between Parentheses: Essays, Articles, and Speeches, 1998–2003*. Edited by Ignacio Echevarría. Translated by Natasha Wimmer. New York: New Directions, 2011.

———. "Positions Are Positions and Sex Is Sex." [Interview by Eliseo Álvarez. Translated by Sybil Perez.] In *Roberto Bolaño: The Last Interview and Other Conversations*. Translated by Sybil Perez. New York: Melville House, 2009.

Borzutzky, Daniel. *The Book of Interfering Bodies*. New York: Nightboat, 2011.

———. *In the Murmurs of the Rotten Carcass Economy*. New York: Nightboat, 2015.

Carson, Anne. "Every Exit Is an Entrance (A Praise of Sleep)." In *Decreation*. New York: Vintage, 2006.

Cixous, Hélène. "Promised Cities." In *Ex-Cities*. Edited by Aaron Levy and Jean-Michel Rabaté. Translated by Laurent Milesi. Philadelphia: Slough, 2006.

———. "The School of Dreams." In *Three Steps on the Ladder of Writing*. Translated by Sarah Cornell and Susan Sellers. New York: Columbia University Press, 1993.

Deutsche, Rosalyn. *Evictions: Art and Spatial Politics*. Cambridge: MIT Press, 1996.

Duras, Marguerite. "The Death of the Young British Pilot." In *Writing*. Translated by Mark Polizzotti. Minneapolis: University of Minnesota Press, 2011.

El Shakry, Omnia. "Every Sufi Master Is, in a Sense, a Freudian Psychotherapist." Edited by Sam Haselby. *Aeon*. Published April 17, 2018. https://aeon.co/ideas/every-sufi-master-is-a-kind-of -freudian-psychotherapist.

Franck, Karen A. "As Prop and Symbol: Engaging with Works of Art in Public Space." In *The Uses of Art in Public Space*. Edited by Julia Lossau and Quentin Stevens. New York and London: Routledge, 2015.

Freud, Sigmund. *The Interpretation of Dreams*. Translated by James Strachey. New York: Basic, 2010.

Gödde, Christoph, and Henri Lonitz. Editorial Foreword to *Dream Notes* by Theodor W. Adorno. Translated by Rodney Livingstone. Malden, MA: Polity, 2007.

Hejinian, Lyn. "The Rejection of Closure." Poetry Foundation website. Published October 13, 2009. https://www.poetryfoundation.org /articles/69401/the-rejection-of-closure. Previously published in *The Language of Inquiry*. Berkeley: University of California Press, 2000.

hooks, bell. "Choosing the Margin as a Space of Radical Openness." In *Yearning: Race, Gender, and Cultural Politics*. Boston: South End, 1990.

Jasper, David. *The Sacred Desert: Religion, Literature, Art, and Culture*. Malden, MA: Blackwell, 2004.

Jelin, Elizabeth. *State Repression and the Labors of Memory*. Translated by Judy Rein and Marcial Godoy-Anativia. Minneapolis: University of Minnesota Press, 2003.

Jung, C. G. *Dreams*. Translated by R. F. C. Hull. Princeton, NJ: Princeton University Press, 2010.

Kester, Grant H., ed. *Art, Activism, and Oppositionality: Essays from Afterimage*. Durham: Duke University Press, 1998.

Lispector, Clarice. *Água Viva*. Translated by Stefan Tobler. New York: New Directions, 2012.

López-Calvo, Ignacio, ed. *Roberto Bolaño: A Less Distant Star*. New York: Palgrave Macmillan, 2015.

Nelson, Maggie. *Jane: A Murder*. Berkeley, CA: Soft Skull, 2005.

Notley, Alice. "Dreams, Again." In *Talisman: A Journal of Contemporary Poetry and Poetics*. Issue 42, 2014.

Ogden, Thomas H. *Conversations at the Frontier of Dreaming*. Lanham, MD: Jason Aronson, 2001.

Pippin, Tina. *Apocalyptic Bodies: The Biblical End of the World in Text and Image*. London and New York: Routledge, 1999.

Rahnavard, Zahra. "If a Nation Wants to Change Its Destiny . . ." [Interview by Kaleme.com.] In *The People Reloaded: The Green Movement and the Struggle for Iran's Future*. Edited by Nader Hashemi and Danny Postel. Brooklyn, NY: Melville House, 2011.

Scenters-Zapico, Natalie. *The Verging Cities*. Fort Collins, CO: Center for Literary Publishing, 2015.

Stauffer, Jill. *Ethical Loneliness: The Injustice of Not Being Heard*. New York: Columbia University Press, 2015.

Tulli, Magdalena. *Dreams and Stones*. Translated by Bill Johnston. New York: Archipelago, 2004.

Waldman, Anne. "In April." In *Journals and Dreams*. New York: Stonehill, 1976.

Zebracki, Martin. "Art Engagers: What Does Public Art Do to Its Publics? The Case of the 'Butt Plug Gnome.'" In *The Uses of Art in Public Space*. Edited by Julia Lossau and Quentin Stevens. New York and London: Routledge, 2015.

Permissions

Acknowledgments

The women and men whose (hi)stories are detailed in this book, in order of appearance:

Alireza Sabouri Miandehi
Behnam Ganji
Nahal Sahabi
Maryam Soudbar Athatan
Seyed Ali Habibi Mousavi Khameneh
Sattar Beheshti
Fatemeh Rajabpour Chokami and Sorour Boroumand Chokami
Parisa Keli
Kasra Sharafi
Abdoulreza Soudbakhsh
Ahmad Nejati Kargar
Shabnam Sohrabi

The information on their deaths has been compiled from the following sources: Aleph.org; BBC Persian; Behesht-e Zahra Cemetery website; Center for Human Rights in Iran (persian .iranhumanrights.org), including the radio program *5 in the Afternoon; Daily Mail;* DW Persian; *Exile Activist* blog on WordPress (exilesactivist.wordpress.com); Facebook; Fars News; *Free Index* blog on Blogspot; Google Images; Gooya News; the *Guardian;* Hamshahri Online; Human Rights Activists News Agency (hra-news.org/fa); Irangreenvoice.com; the *Iranian* (iranian.com); Iranian Students News Agency (isna); IranianUK (iranianuk.com); Islamic Revolution Document Center (irdc.ir); Jaras website (rahesabz.net); Kaleme.com; kanoon-jb.blogsky.com; *Khabar Online;* Mashregh News; Nahal Sahabi's blog on Blogfa (nahal53.blogfa.com); Omid Memorial by Boroumand Center website (iranrights.org/fa/memorial); Persianblog.ir, including images; *PersianReflection* blog on Blogfa; Peykeiran.com; *Pink Sado* blog on Blogspot; Radio Farda website, including *Victims of 88* series; Radio Zamaneh website; Raja News; Rooz Online; Serat News; Soundcloud, including audio files of interviews with survivors; Tabnak News Agency; Tehran University of Medical Sciences, public relations page (pr.tums.ac.ir); *Victims of 88* documentary film on Manoto TV; VOA Persian; Wikipedia; and YouTube audio files and videos.

Working through these sources, one, unfortunately, notices many gaps, inconsistencies, and—more often than not—even contradictory information. Some sources are more reliable than others, and in some cases, webpages used to gather information may have even ceased to exist. The premise of this work, however, has been to live within this very chaos, trying to make sense of what one has experienced and inherited.

The narrative of the city of Tehran owes its existence to the many sources of inspiration within it: its public and private spaces, as well as its residents: strangers, acquaintances, family, and friends who became characters in the novel. Most artworks appearing in this layer are also real artworks or fictionalized versions of real artworks, whose titles and artists I've decided to not name for safety reasons. I am indebted to all for giving life to this world. The dream circles are hand drawn by Sara Dolatabadi, based on software-generated word clouds.

I am grateful for the intellectual and psychological support of many people, living and dead, who were by my side, physically or spiritually, through the long years of writing this book. Since I feel it's best to refrain from naming the Iranian ones, I've decided to not name the others either. You know who you are. Thank you for being there. I couldn't have done it without you.

I want to end by invoking Mir-Hossein Mousavi. He has honored his pledge to the people and their rights since 2009, and has, with his wife, Zahra Rahnavard, and Mehdi Karroubi, been under house arrest since 2011. As Mousavi once said, "Hope is the seed of our identity." This book is my share of a collective attempt to care for that seed, the seed that keeps growing in and with the body of Iran, even if I am far away from it.

Coffee House Press began as a small letterpress operation in 1972 and has grown into an internationally renowned nonprofit publisher of literary fiction, essay, poetry, and other work that doesn't fit neatly into genre categories.

Coffee House is both a publisher and an arts organization. Through our *Books in Action* program and publications, we've become interdisciplinary collaborators and incubators for new work and audience experiences. Our vision for the future is one where a publisher is a catalyst and connector.

LITERATURE
is not the same thing as
PUBLISHING

Funder Acknowledgments

Coffee House Press is an internationally renowned independent book publisher and arts nonprofit based in Minneapolis, MN; through its literary publications and *Books in Action* program, Coffee House acts as a catalyst and connector—between authors and readers, ideas and resources, creativity and community, inspiration and action.

Coffee House Press books are made possible through the generous support of grants and donations from corporations, state and federal grant programs, family foundations, and the many individuals who believe in the transformational power of literature. This activity is made possible by the voters of Minnesota through a Minnesota State Arts Board Operating Support grant, thanks to the legislative appropriation from the Arts and Cultural Heritage Fund. Coffee House also receives major operating support from the Amazon Literary Partnership, Jerome Foundation, McKnight Foundation, Target Foundation, and the National Endowment for the Arts (NEA). To find out more about how NEA grants impact individuals and communities, visit www.arts.gov.

Coffee House Press receives additional support from the Elmer L. & Eleanor J. Andersen Foundation; the David & Mary Anderson Family Foundation; Bookmobile; Dorsey & Whitney LLP; Foundation Technologies; Fredrikson & Byron, P.A.; the Fringe Foundation; Kenneth Koch Literary Estate; the Matching Grant Program Fund of the Minneapolis Foundation; Mr. Pancks' Fund in memory of Graham Kimpton; the Schwab Charitable Fund; Schwegman, Lundberg & Woessner, P.A.; the Silicon Valley Community Foundation; and the U.S. Bank Foundation.

The Publisher's Circle of Coffee House Press

Publisher's Circle members make significant contributions to Coffee House Press's annual giving campaign. Understanding that a strong financial base is necessary for the press to meet the challenges and opportunities that arise each year, this group plays a crucial part in the success of Coffee House's mission.

Recent Publisher's Circle members include many anonymous donors, Suzanne Allen, Patricia A. Beithon, the E. Thomas Binger & Rebecca Rand Fund of the Minneapolis Foundation, Andrew Brantingham, Robert & Gail Buuck, Dave & Kelli Cloutier, Louise Copeland, Jane Dalrymple-Hollo & Stephen Parlato, Mary Ebert & Paul Stembler, Kaywin Feldman & Jim Lutz, Chris Fischbach & Katie Dublinski, Sally French, Jocelyn Hale & Glenn Miller, the Rehael Fund-Roger Hale/Nor Hall of the Minneapolis Foundation, Randy Hartten & Ron Lotz, Dylan Hicks & Nina Hale, William Hardacker, Randall Heath, Jeffrey Hom, Carl & Heidi Horsch, the Amy L. Hubbard & Geoffrey J. Kehoe Fund, Kenneth & Susan Kahn, Stephen & Isabel Keating, Julia Klein, the Kenneth Koch Literary Estate, Cinda Kornblum, Jennifer Kwon Dobbs & Stefan Liess, the Lambert Family Foundation, the Lenfestey Family Foundation, Joy Linsday Crow, Sarah Lutman & Rob Rudolph, the Carol & Aaron Mack Charitable Fund of the Minneapolis Foundation, George & Olga Mack, Joshua Mack & Ron Warren, Gillian McCain, Malcolm S. McDermid & Katie Windle, Mary & Malcolm McDermid, Sjur Midness & Briar Andresen, Daniel N. Smith III & Maureen Millea Smith, Peter Nelson & Jennifer Swenson, Enrique & Jennifer Olivarez, Alan Polsky, Marc Porter & James Hennessy, Robin Preble, Alexis Scott, Ruth Stricker Dayton, Jeffrey Sugerman & Sarah Schultz, Nan G. & Stephen C. Swid, Kenneth Thorp in memory of Allan Kornblum & Rochelle Ratner, Patricia Tilton, Joanne Von Blon, Stu Wilson & Melissa Barker, Warren D. Woessner & Iris C. Freeman, and Margaret Wurtele.

For more information about the Publisher's Circle and other ways to support Coffee House Press books, authors, and activities, please visit www.coffeehousepress.org/pages/support or contact us at info@coffeehousepress.org.

Poupeh Missaghi is a writer, a translator both into and out of Persian, *Asymptote*'s Iran editor-at-large, and an educator. She holds a doctorate in creative writing from the University of Denver, a master's degree in creative writing from Johns Hopkins University, and a master's degree in translation studies from Azad University, Tehran. Her nonfiction, fiction, and translations have appeared in numerous journals, and she has several books of translation published in Iran. She is currently a visiting assistant professor at the Department of Writing at the Pratt Institute, Brooklyn.

trans(re)lating house one was designed by Bookmobile Design & Digital Publisher Services. Text is set in Miller Text.